— A *Caroline* MYSTERY —

TRAITOR IN THE SHIPYARD

Enjoy all of these American Girl Mysteries®:

THE SILENT STRANGER   A *Kaya* Mystery

LADY MARGARET'S GHOST   A *Felicity* Mystery

SECRETS IN THE HILLS   A *Josefina* Mystery

THE RUNAWAY FRIEND   A *Kirsten* Mystery

THE HAUNTED OPERA   A *Marie-Grace* Mystery

THE CAMEO NECKLACE   A *Cécile* Mystery

SHADOWS ON SOCIETY HILL   An *Addy* Mystery

CLUE IN THE CASTLE TOWER   A *Samantha* Mystery

THE CRYSTAL BALL   A *Rebecca* Mystery

MISSING GRACE   A *Kit* Mystery

CLUES IN THE SHADOWS   A *Molly* Mystery

LOST IN THE CITY   A *Julie* Mystery

and many more!

— A *Caroline* MYSTERY —

TRAITOR IN THE SHIPYARD

by Kathleen Ernst

✦ American Girl®

For Peg, in honor of fifteen shared adventures

Published by American Girl Publishing
Copyright © 2013 by American Girl

Questions or comments? Call 1-800-845-0005, visit **americangirl.com**,
or write to Customer Service, American Girl, 8400 Fairway Place,
Middleton, WI 53562-0497.

Printed in China
13 14 15 16 17 18 LEO 10 9 8 7 6 5 4 3 2 1

PICTURE CREDITS
The following individuals and organizations have generously
given permission to reprint illustrations contained in "Looking Back":
pp. 174–175—Picture Collection, The New York Public Library,
Astor, Lenox and Tilden Foundations (girl delivering gunpowder); courtesy
of the U.S. Naval Academy Museum (warships); pp. 176–177—New York State
Office of Parks, Recreation and Historic Preservation, Bureau of Historic Sites
(harbor scene); U.S. National Archives (*General Pike*); © Richard Cummins/Corbis
(barrel); pp. 178–179—courtesy of the William L. Clements Library, University
of Michigan (secret message); with permission of the Royal Ontario Museum
© ROM (spy's map); pp. 180–181—Library and Archives Canada, Acc. No.
C-011053, detail (Laura Secord); Library and Archives Canada, Acc. No. C-115424,
detail (African American family); courtesy of the National Park Service, Fort
McHenry National Monument and Shrine, Artist: Keith Rocco (African American
sailor); p. 182—courtesy of the Ohio Historical Society, SC 1038, AL00195.

Illustrations by Sergio Giovine

Cataloging-in-Publication data
available from the Library of Congress

TABLE OF CONTENTS

1

A STRANGER ARRIVES

Caroline Abbott found it hard to keep
from humming a cheerful tune, even though
she was dusting. *Don't disturb Papa while he's
working,* she reminded herself. Her father built
ships, and she loved spending time with him
in the shipyard office. But today, being here
with him seemed especially precious. She was
spending much of the summer helping her
cousin's family on their distant farm. She'd
come home to enjoy yesterday's Independence
Day celebration, but soon she would return to
her relatives' farm.

"Caroline," Papa called. "I need you to run
an errand for me."

"Of course, Papa!" She dropped her dust cloth
and hurried across the room to his big desk.

Papa handed her a folded piece of paper. "Please deliver this progress report to the navy shipyard."

"I will." As Caroline tucked Papa's note into her pocket, she studied his design sketch for a schooner. Ever since the United States had declared war on Great Britain more than a year ago, Abbott's Shipyard had produced gunboats for the navy. Caroline was proud that her family's business helped defend her village of Sackets Harbor, New York—and all of mighty Lake Ontario. The gunboats were heavy, though, with none of the graceful lines of the schooners and sloops her father had designed before the war.

"I'm glad the navy asked you to build a schooner," she told him. She imagined the pretty ship slipping through marshes, hiding behind islands, pouncing on small British ships sailing foolishly close to the American side of the great lake. "It will be lovely!"

"I think so." Papa surveyed the design. "But whether a gunboat or a schooner, what the navy

2

men want most is a speedy ship, quickly built.
I wish we weren't shorthanded."

Caroline nodded. Two of their workers had
recently enlisted in the American navy.

"Run along now." Papa kissed her forehead.
"Deliver my message only to someone you
know. There may be spies about."

Caroline hated the idea that any stranger
she passed on the street might be a British spy!
"I'll be careful," she promised.

Outside, she paused to watch the carpenters
who were finishing the skeletal wooden frame
for the new schooner. The day was sticky-hot,
and the men labored with sleeves rolled up and
hats pulled low to shade their eyes. The yard
thrummed with the sounds of saws and axes
and mallets, shouts and whistles and snatches
of song.

As Caroline headed to the street, she jumped
on a log and started to walk its length, arms
outstretched. She had almost reached the end
when someone called, "Miss Caroline!"

Caroline glanced up and smiled. "Good day,

Hosea!" Hosea Barton was Abbott's sailmaker. He was a tall man with brown skin, a soft voice, and long fingers that worked huge pieces of heavy sailcloth with ease.

He doffed his felt hat. "I didn't mean to interrupt your play."

"You didn't," she assured him. "I'm on my way to the navy yard."

"It's nice to see you having fun for once," Hosea said.

His observation made her feel good. Since the war had begun, she'd helped at home, helped at her cousin's farm, helped at the shipyard. She'd even helped defend Abbott's during a British attack!

"I try to do my part," she said, "but my friend Rhonda and I find time for games, too. We like to play jackstraws or dominoes, and sometimes we race hoops." The two girls had decided to make a quilt, too. Since Caroline loved to sew, she was excited about that project.

Hosea's eyes twinkled. "And now that *Miss Caroline* is seaworthy again," he said, "I expect you'll be having fun on the lake."

Caroline grinned. *Miss Caroline* was her skiff. In May she'd sunk the skiff across the mouth of a creek to keep a British ship from catching an American supply boat. She'd thought the skiff was gone for good, but Papa had surprised her by raising it and making repairs. He'd presented her with the skiff just the day before. She could hardly wait to get back out on the lake!

"Papa said Rhonda and I may take the skiff out by ourselves," she told Hosea, "but we need a day when the wind is not too gentle and not too strong."

"I hope that day comes quickly," Hosea said. "Everyone needs to forget about the war from time to time. Especially right now."

Following his gaze, Caroline saw an American warship patrolling in the distance— a reminder that the British colony of Upper Canada was just across the lake. Before the war, Caroline and her family had often gone there to shop or visit relatives. Now, it was enemy territory.

Closer to shore, two almost-finished boats floated in the harbor. Abbott's workers were fitting a mast into place on their latest gunboat. Nearby, workers on the navy's newest warship, *General Pike*, were rigging up the lines that would control the sails. Guards stood on the deck.

"Have you heard when *General Pike* will be ready?" she asked. Once complete, the frigate would be the mightiest vessel ever to sail Lake Ontario.

"The sails aren't finished." Hosea glanced over his shoulder, as if making sure that no one else could hear. "The navy is also waiting for a shipment of gunpowder. With twenty-eight cannons aboard, *General Pike* needs ten thousand pounds."

"Gracious!" Caroline was so startled that she lost her balance and had to jump down from the log.

"And until *Pike* launches, the British rule the lake." Hosea looked frustrated. "It's maddening to see our fleet bottled up here to protect

6

General Pike while British ships cruise about Lake Ontario at will."

"Papa says the navy's most important job right now is protecting *General Pike*," she said.

Hosea nodded. "Our enemies want desperately to seize or destroy *Pike* before it ever sets sail. If that happens, the war on the Great Lakes will be lost."

Caroline looked back over the harbor. If the Americans couldn't get *General Pike* into service soon, they might not be able to defend themselves.

Then she lifted her chin. "Well," she said briskly, "when our gunboat and schooner are finished, the navy will have two more vessels to keep an eye on the British. Are you making the schooner's sails?"

"They are well under way," he assured her. "Have you met Paul, my new apprentice?"

She nodded. "I met him yesterday at the Independence Day picnic. He doesn't look much older than I am!"

"I don't think he is," Hosea said. "When

I asked your papa for an apprentice, I knew it might not be easy to find one. With so many men in the army or navy, most families need their boys to help at home. Paul's an orphan, though. He's been on his own for years."

How dreadful, Caroline thought. She tried to imagine how she would feel if left to wander and make her way alone. She didn't like that picture, not at all. "I'm glad Paul's found a good place to settle, where he can learn a trade," she told Hosea. "And with him being so close to my own age, I expect we'll become good friends."

Hosea said, "You come by the sail loft and visit, Miss Caroline. Paul is very shy, but he'd probably enjoy the chance to talk with someone his own age." He wiped sweat from his forehead with a kerchief. "I'll let you be on your way."

The navy shipyard was right next to Abbott's, but it took Caroline several minutes to reach the gate. In the past year, thousands of people had moved to Sackets Harbor—shipbuilders, tavern keepers, merchants, and the sailors, soldiers, and marines sent to guard the shipyards and fight the British. The streets were always jammed.

After worming her way to the navy yard, she explained her errand to the guards, who let her pass. Caroline found Mr. Eckford, the master shipbuilder, working in his office with his clerk. Mr. Eckford was a dark-haired man with side whiskers that reached his chin.

"I've a report from my father," she said.

Mr. Eckford read the note. "It sounds as if the schooner is coming right along. My compliments to your father."

"I'll tell him, sir," Caroline said.

"Mr. Crowley?" Mr. Eckford handed the note to his clerk. "Please make a copy of this to send to the naval officers. Put the original with the Abbott's contract."

Mr. Crowley was a small man with hunched shoulders, spectacles perched low on his nose, and a constant frown. "Thundering thieves," the clerk grumbled under his breath. "As if I didn't already have ten things to do at once."

Caroline didn't want to linger. "Good day,

Mr. Eckford," she said. "And good day to you too, Mr. Crowley." She pronounced the clerk's name carefully, because in her mind she called him "Mr. *Growl*-y." She liked talking with him, though, because his complaints often held phrases—like "thundering thieves"—that made her smile.

Mr. Crowley shrugged and went back to his work. Caroline turned to go.

"Miss Caroline, there's one more thing." Mr. Eckford's face grew serious. "Please tell your father that we caught a spy in the yard yesterday."

Caroline caught her breath. *"Inside* the yard?"

The shipbuilder pounded a fist against his palm. "The black-hearted wretch was looking for weak spots in our defenses."

Hosea is right, she thought. *The British are desperate to steal or destroy the mighty frigate.* "Thank goodness the spy was caught," she said.

"Remind your father to be on his guard," Mr. Eckford said. "Someone might try to sneak into Abbott's as well, looking for information about the ships being built there."

Caroline's stomach knotted as she imagined a spy surveying Abbott's Shipyard. *Blast this war!* she thought. *None of us can rest until the British are sent home to Upper Canada for good.*

When Caroline got back to Abbott's, she spotted Hosea's apprentice, Paul, in the shipyard. He was a skinny boy with curly hair the color of molasses. He walked with hands in his pockets, head down, shoulders hunched.

Caroline called, "Good morning, Paul!"

He jerked to a halt, clearly startled. "Why... that is..." His cheeks grew red. "I mean to say, good morning, miss."

Caroline joined him. "I hope you're enjoying your work here," she said with her friendliest smile.

Paul opened his mouth, then closed it again. His gaze flitted from the ground to the workshops to the schooner.

Gracious! she thought. *He **is** shy.* She imagined that a boy who'd been taking care of himself for years didn't have much practice making friends. "I know Hosea is glad to have your help," she added, trying to put him at ease.

"I—I do aim to be helpful," Paul stammered. "I'm needed in the loft now." With a quick nod, he turned away.

Caroline watched him go. Paul might *need* a friend, but he didn't seem to know how to go about making one. Perhaps knowing that she was the master shipbuilder's daughter made Paul feel especially shy. She would have to think of a way to let Paul know that she truly wanted him to be content at Abbott's.

She hurried on to the office, where she found Mr. Tate, the chief carpenter, huddled with Papa. "... a question about the keel, here," Mr. Tate was saying as he pointed at Papa's sketch. The keel was a long wooden beam at the schooner's bottom.

"Ah." Papa nodded. "That is a new design. Let me explain my thinking." He spread a more detailed drawing on the desk, pinning the corners down with stones.

"Pardon me," Caroline said. "I have news from Mr. Eckford." She quickly told the men about the spy caught in the navy yard.

Papa looked at Mr. Tate. "The workers must be alert while on guard duty, especially at night. No doubt the British would like to steal our designs or destroy our gunboat and schooner."

"Yes, sir," Mr. Tate said. He gave Caroline a reassuring look. "Never fear, miss. No one will harm *our* ships if the workers have anything to say about it."

Mr. Tate had worked at Abbott's for many years, and his reminder made Caroline feel a little better. Even more comforting, though, was hearing Papa's voice as he and Mr. Tate got back to work. The British had captured Papa when the war began. They'd held him as a prisoner for many anxious months. He hadn't been home for long, and it still seemed like a miracle to have him back. But until the war ended, Papa—and the family business—remained in danger.

Someone passed by the front window, throwing a shadow into the room. Caroline hurried to the door and cracked it open.

The visitor, who was raising his hand to knock, blinked in surprise and snatched the sweat-stained hat from his head. Faded trousers and linen shirt and vest marked him as a civilian, not a military man. He had blue eyes and black hair, and the weathered face of a man who spent time outdoors.

"May I help you?" Caroline asked in a polite but low voice. She didn't want to disturb her father and Mr. Tate unless it was necessary.

The stranger stared at her. "Bless my soul," he said. "You're Caroline!"

2
MR. OSBORNE'S TALE

Caroline blinked at the stranger. How did this man know her name? "Yes, I'm Caroline," she said. She wanted to add, *Who are **you**?* It didn't seem polite, though.

Papa's footsteps sounded behind her. As Caroline stepped aside, her father gasped. For a long moment, Papa and the newcomer stared at each other in silence. Then Papa wiped a hand over his eyes. "Cyrus Osborne. Is it truly you?"

"It is." Mr. Osborne smiled. "Hello, old friend."

Papa looked dazed. "I was told that you were dead!"

"Let me guess," Mr. Osborne said. "Did Private McGivens give you that news?"

Mr. Tate glanced at Caroline with a question in his eyes: *Who is it?* She gave him a tiny, bewildered shrug: *I don't know.*

"You should have known better than to believe McGivens," Mr. Osborne was saying. "He enjoyed making prisoners miserable."

Prisoners? Caroline wondered. Papa must have met Mr. Osborne while being held in Upper Canada. Private McGivens had likely been one of the British guards.

"Cyrus Osborne," Papa repeated, his voice husky. The two men shook hands and thumped each other on the back. When Papa stepped away, his eyes looked damp.

Then Papa drew Caroline forward. "Daughter, allow me to present a very good friend. Mr. Osborne and I were prisoners together."

"How do you do, sir," Caroline said.

Papa introduced Mr. Tate, who shook hands with the visitor. "I'll come back later, sir," Mr. Tate told Papa. "I have everything I need for the time being." He left the office.

Papa glanced at the clock on a high shelf.

"It's almost noon. I usually eat here, Cy, but I'd like to get away from work so we can talk. Caroline, do you know what your mama and grandmother have planned for dinner?"

"Beans and bacon," Caroline told him. "With biscuits and salad greens as well. There will be plenty."

Papa looked at Mr. Osborne. "I want you to meet the rest of my family. Have you eaten yet?"

"No, I just arrived in town this morning." Mr. Osborne's warm smile included Caroline. "It would be my pleasure to dine with your family."

Caroline led Papa and their guest from the yard to the busy main street, slipping among the crowds, carefully avoiding the supply wagons and travelers on horseback in the streets. "It's not far," she told Mr. Osborne.

The Abbotts' frame house perched on a hill overlooking the harbor. Caroline loved her home—her small bedroom facing the lake, the tidy vegetable garden she helped tend, the fragrant kitchen and gracious parlor. She loved hearing Papa's footsteps in the hall each morning, and the murmur of Mama's voice, and the sound of Grandmother's knife chopping vegetables.

Once inside, Papa called Mama and Grandmother from the kitchen. "One of the guards told me that Cyrus had been shot while trying to escape," he explained, "so you can imagine my feelings when he presented himself!"

Mama's face lit with delight. "We rejoice in your safe return to New York, sir," she said.

"My wife managed Abbott's while I was gone, and did a fine job," Papa added. "She still helps with the accounts."

Caroline beamed at her mother. She was proud of everything Mama had accomplished.

Papa gestured to Grandmother. "And my mother-in-law, Mrs. Livingston."

Grandmother was a small woman who leaned on a cane and often struggled with aches and pains. She was also one of the bravest and most capable people Caroline had ever met—and a good judge of character.

Now Grandmother surveyed their guest and

gave one quick, approving nod. "I'm glad to hear that you managed to evade those wretched British," she said, "but it looks as if you have not yet caught up on meals. Caroline, set extra places at the table." She made a shooing gesture with her hands.

Caroline laid out forks, knives, mugs, and pewter plates for Papa and his friend. "Here you are, sir," she told Mr. Osborne. "It's just the family today. The Hathaways—our boarders— are visiting friends."

Once everyone was settled and the food had been served, Caroline was eager to hear more from their guest. "Please, Mr. Osborne, will you tell us how you were captured? What did you do before the war?"

Mr. Osborne spread blackberry jam on a biscuit. "I was raised on a farm about twenty miles from here. When the war began, I was working the farm with my elderly father. I was married once, but only briefly. My wife died of fever."

The grief in his eyes made Caroline's heart

19

ache. *He must have loved his wife very much*, she thought.

Then Mr. Osborne gave a tiny shake, as if ridding himself of sad memories. "I have some skill at making chairs, which helped earn money during lean times on the farm. One day, soon after the war was declared, I traveled to Upper Canada to deliver some chairs." He spread his hands, palms up. "The British thought that I was a spy who'd come to gain information about the ships they were building, or how many ships were in their fleet."

"The British think they can arrest anyone they please," Caroline muttered.

Papa said, "For several weeks, the British held Cyrus and me in the same prison room in the fort at Kingston."

"We quickly became good friends," Mr. Osborne continued, "but as you know, when the British have more prisoners than they can handle, they move men east. I was put on a ship headed for the Atlantic coast. One night I was able to escape."

"Just as Papa did!" Caroline exclaimed.

Mr. Osborne nodded. "But while trying to make my way home through the Canadian wilderness, I became quite ill. I managed to reach good friends who still live in British territory, and they kept me hidden and nursed me back to health. Months passed before I was able to slip back to New York."

"Your father must have been overjoyed to see you," Mama said.

Another shadow darkened Mr. Osborne's eyes. "My father died while I was gone."

So much sadness, Caroline thought. "What about your farm?" she asked anxiously.

"My younger brother and his family had taken charge," Mr. Osborne told her. "They welcomed me joyfully. Still . . . it seemed as if I'd become almost a—a farmhand on the land I'd once managed."

"What brings you to Sackets Harbor?" Grandmother asked.

"Well, I wanted to see if John had managed to get home." Mr. Osborne looked at Papa.

"And I've decided to start fresh in a place where no one knows me."

"Are you looking for a job?" Papa's face lit up. "How about working at the shipyard?"

Mr. Osborne looked startled. "I know nothing about building ships!"

"You have some carpentry skills." Papa waved a hand, dismissing his friend's concern. "My men can train you."

"Papa's crew is short two carpenters," Caroline added.

Mr. Osborne looked down, as if struggling to reach a decision. Then he grinned—a true, broad grin that drove the lingering sadness from his eyes. "Very well! I accept your kind offer. Perhaps there's a vacant corner at the shipyard where I might curl up at night?"

"Certainly." Papa nodded. "Several of the men sleep there. They take turns standing watch."

"I'll help with that too," Mr. Osborne offered.

Papa looked relieved. "Thank you, Cy. There are spies in Sackets Harbor, and protecting the shipyard is a constant worry. I'm grateful for your help." He grinned. "And perhaps we can find time for another game of checkers."

Caroline exchanged a delighted look with her mother. She could tell from Papa's face that nothing would please him more than spending time with his friend.

That evening, Mr. Osborne returned to the house for supper. Afterward Caroline and her friend Rhonda Hathaway washed up, letting the adults visit in the parlor. Rhonda's little sister, Amelia, put the dishes away.

Grandmother joined them as they finished. "Amelia, I'm going to make a nice pudding."

"I'll help!" Amelia said at once. She ran to fetch her apron.

Grandmother turned to the older girls. "Did I hear you say you're ready to start your quilt?"

"Yes," Caroline said. "We've collected enough scraps of fabric."

"We just need to choose a design," Rhonda added.

Grandmother smiled. "You two run along, then."

Rhonda and Caroline went upstairs to their bedroom. Caroline began pulling cloth from her worktable. Some scraps were no bigger than her palm. A few pieces were a yard or more in length. Soon the bed was covered with fabric.

"We have a decision to make," Rhonda said. "Who will own the finished quilt? We won't be able to share it. When the war ends, the army will send my father somewhere else and we'll leave Sackets Harbor."

Caroline didn't like to think about saying good-bye to her friend. "I had an idea about the quilt," she said. "Shall we make it as a gift for Lydia?" Caroline's cousin Lydia and her parents had stayed in the Abbotts' home the previous winter after fleeing from Upper Canada, so Rhonda knew her well.

"I love that idea!" Rhonda beamed. "I miss Lydia."

"Their new cabin needs cheerful things," Caroline added. When Lydia and her parents had escaped Upper Canada, they'd had to leave most of their belongings behind. After Caroline had arrived at her cousin's new farm a few weeks ago, she'd suggested that she and Lydia make a quilt. She had quickly discovered, though, that farm chores took up every minute of daylight.

"What pattern should we use?" Rhonda asked. "I like the Nine Patch." This pattern was simple but quite pretty. Nine small squares were sewn together to make a colorful block. When enough Nine Patch blocks were finished, they were sewn together to make a complete quilt top.

"I think we should make a patriotic quilt," Caroline said. "A star pattern might remind people of the stars in our flag. Or ... I know! Maybe we could design a ship pattern."

Rhonda considered that idea. "A ship would be perfect for Sackets Harbor," she allowed, "but it would be challenging to stitch."

"Well, how about this?" Caroline countered. "We can make one big ship block for the center, and surround it with Nine Patch blocks. That way *most* of the quilt will be simple to sew."

"Perfect," Rhonda said happily. "We'll still need help designing the ship, though. And since our mothers and your grandmother are so busy—" She broke off as Caroline's black cat jumped onto the bed. He curled up on a pile of red fabric and began licking one paw.

"Inkpot," Caroline protested, "we need that cloth!"

He paused, giving her a look that seemed to say *I'm using it right now, you silly girl.* Then he returned to his bath.

Caroline laughed. "All right, Inkpot. Rhonda, let's go downstairs and start heating the irons." As she led the way back down to the kitchen, Caroline felt more and more excited about the quilt.

The girls got a good start on ironing their fabric before sundown. When Caroline headed upstairs for bed, she heard Papa's low chuckle from the parlor. "Clever move, my friend," he said.

Mr. Osborne must have agreed to play a game of checkers before he returns to the shipyard for the night, Caroline thought. She smiled as she tiptoed up the steps.

In the bedroom, she found Rhonda brushing her long hair.

"Mr. Osborne seems nice," Rhonda said.

Caroline reached for her nightgown. "Yes indeed. It's wonderful to hear Papa laughing with his friend," she said. The past year had been so difficult for Papa! He'd endured many long months as a prisoner. He'd almost died while trying to get back to Sackets Harbor, and his homecoming had been cut short by a battle. Now he worried constantly about safeguarding the shipyard from spies and possible British attacks.

The British had already attacked Sackets

Harbor twice. They had not won—but next time, that could change. Caroline shivered as she imagined British soldiers and sailors cheering and laughing after destroying all the ships and military supplies at Sackets Harbor. She imagined hearing the faint peal of celebration bells drifting across the lake from Kingston. She imagined British troops and loyalist civilians toasting their success while she and her family and friends were left with nothing but the charred and smoking ruins of the yard, and the wrecks of boats burned to the waterline. All that imagining made her head hurt, and her heart too.

I'm glad Mr. Osborne arrived to help Papa during this dangerous time, Caroline thought. Every man was needed to protect the shipyards! The Americans needed *General Pike*—and Abbott's new gunboat and schooner, too—to win the war.

3
TROUBLE AT THE SHIPYARD

Caroline woke before dawn the next morning. She was disappointed to hear a sharp gust of wind rattle the windowpanes. *No sailing today,* she thought.

She got up anyway. After using the privy out back, she stumbled sleepily into the kitchen. A candle burned on the table, and a low fire flickered in the hearth. Papa was sipping coffee while Mama and Grandmother started breakfast.

"Well, well!" Grandmother said. "Look who's up before the sun."

Caroline tied on her apron. "I wanted a chance to talk to Papa."

"It's come to this, has it?" Papa held out one arm. "My daughter must rise before the roosters just to speak with me?"

Caroline let him pull her close. *He's home,* she told herself. She took pleasure in this simple moment. The kitchen smelled like raspberries stewed with cloves and maple syrup. Mama was humming a hymn.

"Things get so busy during the day," Caroline said finally. "I like this quiet time."

Papa smiled. "I do too."

"How is the schooner coming?" she asked. "Is—"

Someone rapped sharply on the back door. Papa stood. "I'll get it."

A moment later he ushered a grim-faced Mr. Tate inside. Caroline's pleasure drained away like rainwater.

"We have a problem at the yard," Mr. Tate said. "During the night, some scoundrel found planks we'd laid out for the schooner and shoved them into the harbor."

Papa's hands clenched. Caroline's eyes went wide. Who would do such a thing?

"The planks are swollen after soaking in the harbor," Mr. Tate added. "We'll either have to wait for them to dry or shape new ones. Either task will set us back at least a day."

"Wasn't someone on guard?" Caroline asked.

"Jed was." Mr. Tate looked at Papa. "He's most upset, sir. Whoever did this must have slipped the planks into the water while Jed was on the far side of the yard, behind the main buildings."

Papa sighed. "One man can't guard the yard alone in the dark. We'll have to double up."

But asking the men to double up on guard duty will set the work back even further, Caroline thought.

After Mr. Tate left, Grandmother positioned a griddle over the fire. "I'll get breakfast on the table quickly," she told Papa. "I know you'll want to get to the yard. Caroline, will you make the pancakes?"

"Yes, Grandmother," Caroline said. Her voice trembled.

Papa put one finger under her chin and tipped her face up so that he could look her in the eye. "Never fear," he said quietly. "Mr. Tate and I will strengthen the guard detail at Abbott's."

His quiet determination made Caroline feel

a *little* better ... but nothing could change the fact that some troublemaker had crept into her family's shipyard in the dark of night.

When Caroline went to Abbott's that afternoon, she found Mama alone in the office, bent over a big ledger. "Is there anything I can help you with?" Caroline asked.

Mama jotted a figure into a column. "Thank you, Caroline, but what I need most is time to finish these accounts." She dipped her pen into the inkwell.

Caroline slipped back outside and walked toward the schooner. She saw the planks the men had fished from the harbor, now laid out to dry. Papa and Mr. Tate were examining the ship's wooden skeleton. Papa stood with feet planted wide, one hand on a timber, the other hand gesturing.

"Never mind that trouble with the planks, Miss Caroline."

Caroline jumped, startled to find Hosea at her elbow. "Oh—good morning!" She looked back at the planks. "I just hate thinking about someone sneaking into our shipyard."

"No lasting harm was done," Hosea reminded her. "It's going to be a fine schooner."

"I know," she agreed stoutly. But although she appreciated his attempt to cheer her up, she didn't want to talk about the trouble anymore. "Hosea? I tried to talk with Paul yesterday, but he didn't seem to want to talk to me. I don't suppose he's had many friends."

"That young man's used to fending for himself," Hosea agreed. "But having a friend would do him good. I hope you'll try again."

"Oh, I will," Caroline promised. "I thought that perhaps he'd like to play a game sometime when he isn't working."

The sailmaker grinned. "Now, *that's* an offer Paul will surely appreciate."

After Hosea was on his way, Caroline decided to sit on the dock. It always calmed her to hear the Abbott's men working behind her, and to watch ships move through the harbor, and to look out over Lake Ontario.

Today, someone had gotten there first. "Why, Mr. Osborne!" she said. Papa's friend was sitting cross-legged on the dock, scribbling in a little journal with a pencil.

"Caroline!" He blinked and shut his notebook.

She realized that he might want to be alone. "Pardon me. I didn't mean to disturb you."

He smiled. "You're not. Would you like to join me?"

Caroline lowered herself to the warm boards beside him. "What were you writing?"

"You will likely laugh at my expense," Mr. Osborne said ruefully. "I'm trying to write down everything the experienced men tell me about shipbuilding. I want to learn as swiftly as possible."

"I would never laugh about such things," she protested. "I'm sure you'll learn quickly."

"I hope so," Mr. Osborne said. "I want to reward the trust your father has placed in me." He leaned back on his hands. "I'm already

discovering why your father spoke of his shipyard with such longing."

*And I'm starting to understand why Papa likes
Mr. Osborne so much*, Caroline thought. "I love
the shipyard too," she told him.

He gestured toward the harbor. "There is
something exciting about building ships! Especially now, knowing that they'll be used to help
defeat the British."

Caroline followed his gaze. *General Pike*, the
navy ship, towered so tall that Sackets Harbor
seemed like a child's toy village carved from
wooden blocks. Abbott's new gunboat, although
much smaller, would also help defend against
British attack. She was glad to see that the
gunboat's masts were now installed. Next, men
would add the rigging and sails.

"When the men start making a new boat,"
Mr. Osborne mused, "it must be difficult to
find the balance between finishing as quickly
as possible and making sure that everything
works properly."

"Papa and Mr. Tate will take the gunboat on

a trial sail when it's complete," she explained. "They'll make sure that the boat handles well before it's delivered to the navy."

"A trial sail?" Mr. Osborne squinted, as if imagining the scene. "That must be exciting."

She grinned. "Mr. Tate will let some of the workers go out on that first sail. And when the crew returns after a successful trial, they yell and cheer as if it's Independence Day!"

"I was astonished to hear how quickly the gunboat's been built, and *General Pike* too," Mr. Osborne said. "I can't imagine how the workers accomplished such feats!"

"Well, the shipbuilders at both yards are trying new designs," Caroline said. "That gunboat was designed to sail in shallow water, close to shore. The carpenters have learned that it's quicker to fasten the planks with iron spikes instead of the trunnels they used before the war. And instead of using wooden knees, they now—"

"Miss Caroline," Mr. Osborne interrupted, "I beg you to remember that I am new to the business! If you'd be so kind as to tell me what trunnels are, and wooden knees, I might not appear to be a complete simpleton the next time Mr. Tate gives me instructions."

Caroline laughed. "Trunnels are wooden pegs," she explained. "And wooden knees are heavy timbers that help support a ship..."

She and Mr. Osborne chatted until a bell clanged in the yard. "I must get back to work," Mr. Osborne said. "Thank you for your help."

"You're welcome," she assured him. She rarely had the opportunity to tutor anyone about anything! It felt good to have Papa's friend ask for her assistance.

As the clock chimed seven that evening, Rhonda stepped into the shipyard office. "It's getting late!" she told Caroline and Mama. "Your grandmother asked me to buy some fish at the market—and to fetch you home for supper."

"I just finished copying a letter," Caroline told her. "Mama? Are you ready to leave?"

"I'm afraid not," Mama said. "We've got an hour or so of daylight left. Papa and I will likely stay here for a while."

Caroline cleaned the pen and corked the ink-well. Then she and Rhonda left the office. The wind had eased, and midday's glare had faded to a softer light.

"I hope we're not too late to find some nice fish," Rhonda said as they passed under the Abbott's sign.

"Since the war began, the marketplace is never quiet," Caroline reminded her.

As she predicted, they found many sellers still doing a brisk business near the harbor. Farmwives sat by wheelbarrows full of green beans and cucumbers. Peddlers shouted "Sweet raspberries!" or "Fresh ginger cakes!" Caroline loved the whirl of sights and scents and sounds.

She soon spotted two Oneida Indian men crouching by a basket heaped with glassy-eyed trout. "Their fish is always fresh," she said, pointing. She grabbed Rhonda's hand and towed her through the crowd.

They'd almost reached the fish sellers when a burst of laughter rose above the din. "Look!" Rhonda said. "Isn't that Hosea?"

Caroline glanced up and saw Abbott's sailmaker standing nearby with several other black men. Hosea's friends were dressed in the heavy white canvas trousers worn by U.S. Navy sailors. As the girls watched, another black sailor joined the group. This man was short and stocky. He walked with a terrible limp.

"Poor man," Rhonda murmured. "Perhaps he was injured in battle."

"Or maybe he fell from a mast." Caroline sighed. She'd heard many tales about the dangers sailors faced aboard ships. "Well, that man must be a good worker. Otherwise he wouldn't still be in the navy."

She watched Hosea and his friends enter one of the ramshackle taverns squeezed between shops and market stalls. "I'm glad Hosea has some time away from the yard this evening," she added. "Having an apprentice must help a lot."

After purchasing the fish, the girls began making their way through the crowds toward home. "I feel like a fish myself," Caroline said, "struggling upstream!" Rhonda laughed.

As Caroline tried to chart the easiest course, she spotted another familiar face. "Why—there's Mr. Osborne!" A plump, brown-haired lady was walking with him. She wore a lovely yellow-checked dress, a lacy shawl over her shoulders, and a stylish bonnet.

"Who's that?" Rhonda asked.

Caroline shook her head. "I don't recognize her."

When the lady tucked one hand through the crook of Mr. Osborne's elbow, Caroline and Rhonda exchanged a surprised look. "I thought Mr. Osborne didn't know anyone in Sackets Harbor," Rhonda said.

"He said he wanted to come to a place where no one knew him," Caroline agreed.

Rhonda flapped her skirt at a dog sniffing her market basket. "Maybe he's courting that lady and wanted to keep it private."

"But why?" Caroline asked. "He and Papa are close friends. If Mr. Osborne is courting someone in Sackets Harbor, wouldn't he have mentioned it yesterday?"

Rhonda shrugged. "We were just getting acquainted, so perhaps not." She tugged Caroline's arm. "Come along. Your grandmother's waiting."

Ahead of them, Mr. Osborne and his companion turned a corner and disappeared from sight. *Rhonda's right*, Caroline thought. *Mr. Osborne just met most of the family yesterday. Maybe he simply didn't think to mention his lady friend—whoever she is.*

Still, hadn't Mr. Osborne said that he knew nobody in Sackets Harbor except Papa? Caroline couldn't quite shake the uncomfortable feeling prompted by seeing Papa's newly arrived friend strolling through Sackets Harbor with a lady on his arm.

4
SUSPICIONS

"Caroline," Mama said the next morning, "will you walk with Papa and me to the yard? I left Grandmother's lunch basket yesterday, and I'd like you to carry it home again."

"I'd be happy to," Caroline assured her. Overnight thunderstorms had faded to a gray drizzle, so she and Rhonda would not be sailing today. Besides, after all the difficult months when Papa was being held prisoner, she loved simply walking through Sackets Harbor with *both* of her parents. She put on her light hooded cloak, and soon they were on their way.

When they reached the shipyard, one of the men came running. Raindrops dripped from the brim of his hat. He looked miserable. "Mr. Tate said you should come to the sail loft right away,

Mr. Abbott," he panted. "There's more trouble."

"What now?" Papa muttered. Mama and Caroline exchanged a worried glance.

Caroline followed her parents up to the loft, a big room above the office and carpentry shops. They found Mr. Tate and Hosea huddled over a mound of sailcloth. Paul, Hosea's young apprentice, stood nearby, twisting his hands. Mr. Osborne was there as well.

Mr. Tate poked his hand through one of several long gashes in the heavy fabric. "One of the gunboat sails has been slashed, sir."

"How did this *happen*?" Papa demanded. Caroline had never heard him sound so angry.

"Cyrus and I had the first watch last night," Hosea said. "We didn't see or hear a thing. Paul was away, so the loft was empty."

"How long were you gone, Paul?" Papa asked.

Everyone turned to the apprentice. He took a step backward. "I—I don't rightly know, sir," he stammered. His shoulders were stiff, as if he feared a blow. "I only left the yard to—to walk a bit, sir. Stretch my legs." When Paul dared a quick look at Papa, Caroline saw the shine of tears in the boy's eyes. She wondered if Paul had once worked for someone who'd mistreated him.

"All it took was a moment's work," Mr. Tate added quietly. "The truth is, sir, it's impossible for even two men to keep an eye on every corner and cranny of the yard in the pitch-black of a rainy night."

A muscle in Papa's jaw twitched. "Of course," he said. "I did not mean to suggest that the men on guard duty are at fault. Hosea, I want you and Paul to begin repairing the sail at once."

As Caroline followed her parents and Mr. Tate from the loft, she heard Hosea murmur, "Don't fret, lad. We'll get these rips stitched up in no time." She hoped that Hosea, who was always kind and gentle, could convince Paul that he wouldn't be blamed for what had happened.

Caroline plodded down the steps, her mood as gray as the day. *Papa doubled the guard*, she thought. How could a stranger get in and out unnoticed?

They found Mr. Eckford, the navy's master

shipbuilder, and Mr. Crowley, his clerk, waiting in Papa's office. "I sent a man to report the latest damage," Mr. Tate told the Abbotts.

Papa shut the door. Caroline realized that he didn't want any of the workers to overhear their conversation, although she wasn't sure why.

"I'm sorry to hear that you've had more trouble," Mr. Eckford said, rubbing his jaw.

Papa paced the small room. "Someone clearly wants to delay completion of the schooner and the gunboat. What's *not* clear is how the trouble-maker manages to slip in and out of the shipyard without being seen."

Mr. Eckford cleared his throat. "Have you considered that one of your own workers could be doing the damage?"

"No!" Caroline cried. Mama gave her a look that said, *Hush, now.*

Mr. Tate crossed his arms. "I'd vouch for any man in our crew," he told Mr. Eckford.

"I would as well," Papa said.

"Galloping gophers," Mr. Crowley muttered. "How can you be sure? All we've got is a lake to separate New York from Upper Canada."

"Everyone in this area has relatives and friends in Upper Canada, and loyalties aren't always clear," Mr. Eckford agreed. "We know that the British are sending spies to New York, but they are likely getting help from someone here in Sackets Harbor—from an American citizen willing to betray our country."

Caroline stared at him. It was bad enough to worry about British spies creeping about, but a traitor? Someone she *knew*? No. Surely the man causing trouble at Abbott's could not be one of their own trusted workers.

But even as she tried to close her mind to that possibility, a wisp of suspicion slipped in. Most of Abbott's workers had been at the yard for a long time and had proved their loyalty. Most... but not all.

When Caroline returned home, she and Rhonda settled in their bedroom to work on the quilt. Caroline told her friend about the latest trouble at the shipyard. "Papa was very angry."

"I can't blame him!" Rhonda rubbed her arms, as if suddenly chilled.

Caroline watched raindrops roll down the windowpane. "The troublemaker seems to know a lot about the shipyard and the guard schedules," she said. "Most of our workers have been at Abbott's for years." She lowered her voice. "Except for two: Mr. Osborne and Hosea's apprentice, Paul."

Rhonda blinked in surprise. "Paul? I met him on Independence Day—he's just a boy!"

"I know," Caroline admitted. "And he almost cried when he saw the damaged sail. I don't think he could pretend to be that upset."

"As for Mr. Osborne..." Rhonda looked baffled. "You surely don't suspect your father's friend, do you?"

"I don't want to," Caroline whispered. "But— but we didn't have any trouble at the shipyard until *he* arrived. Besides, Papa and Mr. Osborne were together in that British fort for only a few weeks. Papa may not truly know Mr. Osborne very well at all."

Rhonda nibbled her lip, looking troubled.

"And Mr. Osborne said he didn't know anyone here, yet we saw that lady walking on his arm as if they were courting," Caroline added. "What else might he be less than truthful about?"

"I just can't believe it," Rhonda said. She threaded her needle. "Please, let's not talk of such things anymore."

Caroline was ready to turn her thoughts to happier matters too. She reached for a bright square of fabric. For her first quilt block, she'd decided to combine blue and green—colors that reminded her of Lake Ontario, the endless sky above, and the deep woods on shore. She and Rhonda each completed one block before tucking the project away.

To Caroline's surprise, Papa came home at noon. "Your mother suggested that I get away from the yard for a hot meal," he said in a clipped voice. Caroline could tell he was still upset about the trouble at Abbott's.

After everyone was seated, Papa said, "I've invited Mr. Osborne and another guest to visit this evening."

"That's fine," Grandmother assured him. "I'll bake some molasses cakes."

"Who is the second guest, Papa?" Caroline asked.

"Well, it appears that Cyrus has another good friend in Sackets Harbor." Papa's face relaxed. "Yesterday he happened to meet a certain lady who has recently moved to the village."

Rhonda nudged Caroline with her elbow. *See?* her look said. *You were borrowing trouble.*

Caroline shrugged sheepishly, agreeing that she'd been too quick to worry. There *was* a good explanation for Mr. Osborne's lady friend. *And it was no doubt coincidence that the shipyard troubles started just when he arrived in the village, too*, she scolded herself. Gracious, this war was making her as jumpy as a rabbit!

"Cyrus was courting a widow when the war began," Papa was saying. "While he was being held prisoner, she moved to Albany. But after a time in the city, she moved to Sackets Harbor."

Caroline wrinkled her forehead. "Why would she come here?" The village was bursting at the seams!

"Mrs. Hodges—that's her name—is an expert seamstress," Papa explained. "The navy hired her to sew shirts for the sailors, and she managed to find a room to rent."

Caroline was glad to know that Mr. Osborne had unexpectedly found an old friend in Sackets Harbor. *Maybe his luck has turned,* she thought, *and he truly can make a new start here.*

✦

When Caroline returned to Abbott's that afternoon, she found the yard strangely quiet. The workers didn't sing or laugh. *They're worried,* she thought.

Caroline had a small surprise for Paul, so she headed to the sail loft. As she climbed the stairs, she heard Hosea's voice. "... learning so quickly, you need your own sailmaker's palm. I'll help you make one that fits perfectly against your hand. Mark your initials in it, and always keep it with you."

Before stepping into the loft, Caroline knocked politely. "Good afternoon," she called.

Hosea looked up. "Why, come on in, Miss Caroline." He sat on a low bench that kept his tools handy—twine, sharp prickers for making holes in the heavy sailcloth, big needles. Paul sat nearby.

Caroline gestured to the huge sail draped over their laps and across the floor. "Will you be able to mend the sail?"

"Oh, that's already finished," Hosea said. "We got those tears stitched up nice and neat."

"Thank goodness." Caroline looked at Paul, who was sewing with great concentration. "Paul," she said, "I have a gift for you." She pulled from her basket a bundle of wooden sticks, all as thin as a wheat stalk. Mr. Tate had whittled them for her years ago, and she thought Paul might like them.

Paul stared at the sticks. "What are they?"

"Why—they're jackstraws," Caroline said. She put them down beside him. "I thought we could play a game sometime. You drop the jackstraws in a heap on the ground, and we take turns pulling one out *without* moving any of the other pieces."

"Oh," Paul said blankly.

"You'd better start practicing," she advised him, "because I'm pretty good at jackstraws."

Paul finally met Caroline's gaze. His eyes shone with surprise and pleasure, and for a moment Caroline felt as if she'd done something good.

Then his smile faded, and he shook his head. "Thank you, miss, but I—I don't have time for games."

"Now, we won't always be quite so busy," Hosea told Paul. "You'll have time for a bit of play when the schooner's sails are done." Then he sighed. "As long as there's no more trouble causing delays, that is."

Caroline felt like stamping her foot. She

hated knowing that someone who supported the British was sneaking into the shipyard, causing extra work and making Paul feel as if he couldn't stop for a little fun. "I'm so *tired* of this war!" she said crossly.

Hosea tipped his head for a moment, regarding her. Then he said, "Come sit here by me, Miss Caroline."

Perplexed, Caroline pulled up a stool.

Hosea showed her the sailmaker's palm fastened onto his hand. The leather piece nestled against the palm of his hand, with a strap to hold it in place and a hole for his thumb. "I was just reminding Paul how a good sailmaker's palm protects your skin and lets you push with the strength of your whole hand," he said. He slipped his off and handed it to Caroline. "Put this on."

The palm was much too big, but Hosea fastened it as best he could. Then he handed her his needle. "You take the next stitch. Put the needle through right here." He pointed.

Caroline grasped the needle tightly,

positioned it against the sailcloth, and used the heel of her hand—protected by the sailmaker's palm—to push it through. "Like this?"

"Just like that." Hosea nodded. "Now, pull the thread tight before taking another stitch."

With Hosea to guide her, Caroline made a nice line of stitches. "There, Miss Caroline," he said. "When your papa's new schooner is delivered to the navy, your work will be part of it."

Caroline felt a flush of pride. "Thank you for letting me help," she told Hosea. Her anger was gone. *It's just as Grandmother says,* she thought. Taking action always felt better than complaining.

5
STOLEN!

That evening Mr. Osborne brought his friend, Mrs. Lucinda Hodges, to the Abbotts' house. Caroline liked the way their guest's eyes sparkled as Mr. Osborne made the introductions.

"She's very pretty," Rhonda whispered. Mrs. Hodges wore a blue dress, and she'd wrapped a matching scarf around her head—just as ladies in fashion magazines did. Her hair was curled into ringlets that fell over her forehead.

"It's kind of you to invite me into your home," Mrs. Hodges said as everyone moved into the parlor. "I hope you girls will call me 'Miss Lucinda.' 'Mrs. Hodges' always sounds so formal."

"I could have guessed you're a seamstress," Caroline told her. "The pleats on your dress are so fine and even."

"Do you like to sew?" Miss Lucinda asked. She accepted a little cake from a plate that Amelia offered.

"I love to sew!" Caroline said. "Rhonda and I are making a quilt."

Miss Lucinda looked delighted. "May I see?"

Caroline fetched their patchwork blocks and shyly showed them to their guest. "We're just getting started."

"Oh, I do like these color combinations," Miss Lucinda said. "And your stitches are nice and small."

"We hope to sew a picture block for the quilt's center," Rhonda said.

"A ship," Caroline added. "We've never done anything that complicated before, though."

"Would you like help?" Miss Lucinda asked. "If you make a drawing of a ship, I'll show you how to reproduce it with cloth."

Caroline and Rhonda exchanged an excited

glance. "That's very kind," Caroline exclaimed.

Miss Lucinda clapped her hands. "It will be a most welcome diversion from sewing men's shirts, I assure you. How about tomorrow afternoon?"

The girls agreed to visit Miss Lucinda at her boardinghouse. After that, the adults chatted about the war, rising prices, and the difficulty of finding certain goods in the shops. Caroline noticed that Mr. Osborne's gaze seldom left Miss Lucinda. *He seems quite smitten with her,* she thought.

Finally Mr. Osborne said, "Lucinda, I should escort you back to your boardinghouse. I'll be standing watch at the shipyard in a few hours."

"I appreciate your protection, sir, but perhaps I'll do the guiding on the way home." Miss Lucinda looked at the others with mischief dancing in her eyes. "If I'd relied on Mr. Osborne for directions this evening, we'd have gotten quite lost!"

"Now, now," Mr. Osborne protested mildly.

"I arrived in Sackets Harbor just four days ago. You can't expect me to have learned my way around quite yet."

That's not right, Caroline thought. "You mean two days, don't you?" she asked.

Mr. Osborne put his hand to his forehead. "Of course, you're correct. Just *two* days. That provides an even better excuse for the wrong turn I took earlier."

Papa laughed. "You can't get too lost in Sackets Harbor. If your feet get wet, you've gone too far north."

Mr. Osborne chuckled too. Then he gripped Papa's hand. "Thank you for your hospitality, my friend."

After the guests had departed, Caroline and Rhonda got ready for bed. "Miss Lucinda is sweet," Rhonda declared. "I hope she and Mr. Osborne decide to get married."

"I do too," Caroline said slowly, but something was niggling at her. She nudged Inkpot away from her pillow and slipped into bed, trying to decide if she was being silly. Finally she said, "Rhonda? Do you think it was a bit . . . odd for Mr. Osborne to misspeak about how long he's been in Sackets Harbor?"

Rhonda lay down on her pallet. "I'm sure he just got confused."

"It seems strange," Caroline persisted.

"I think you're looking for trouble where none exists," Rhonda said flatly. "This morning you were suspicious because Mr. Osborne hadn't mentioned his lady friend, and that turned out to be nothing at all!"

Caroline sighed. "I suppose all this talk of spies and traitors might have me seeing shadows where none exist," she admitted. "Good night, Rhonda."

Inkpot curled up against Caroline's shoulder, purring. Soon Caroline heard Rhonda's breathing grow deep and rhythmic. Caroline, though, had trouble drifting off. She couldn't quite shake the feeling that Papa's friend was keeping secrets.

Well, perhaps the sewing lesson would be helpful in more ways than one. After all, Miss Lucinda had known Mr. Osborne longer than anyone else in Sackets Harbor. *Maybe,* Caroline thought, *I can learn something more about Mr. Osborne from Miss Lucinda.*

The next morning, Caroline went to the shipyard as soon as household chores were done. Sweat had beaded on her forehead by the time she walked beneath the Abbott's sign. The air felt damp. Even the breeze was fretful, puffing halfheartedly as if too hot and bothered to blow with any spirit. Caroline was starting to fear that she'd be called back to her cousin's farm before she had a chance to sail her skiff at all.

Papa was busy in the office. "Caroline, would you go to the post office and see if a letter has arrived for us? We're waiting to hear from one of our suppliers in Albany."

"Of course," Caroline said. If she couldn't sail, at least she could be useful.

When she reached the post office, Caroline wasn't surprised to find the room crowded.

STOLEN!

Most mail for the village arrived by ship or stagecoach. When letters were delivered, word spread quickly.

The postmaster had dumped what looked to be an entire sack of letters on a table. Homesick sailors, busy merchants, and worried mothers pawed through them. Caroline had to wait her turn in a long line.

When she finally reached the table, she scanned the mail carefully. She found a letter addressed to *Mr. Abbott, Shipmaker, Sackets Harbor* and tucked it away. Just to be sure, she quickly examined the rest of the mail. Good thing! One of the remaining letters was addressed to her.

Caroline snatched it and retreated to a corner. *It's likely from Lydia,* she thought as she opened the letter.

Dear Caroline,

All is well here on the farm. Mama is still away caring for her sister, but our friend Mrs. Parkhurst remains here helping out. Minerva and Garnet are fine. The garden

*is coming along nicely too. I'm afraid I have
completely abandoned the notion of making
a quilt, though. There are too many other
chores to fill my day.*

Your devoted cousin,
Lydia

Caroline blew out a relieved whoosh of
breath. All was well on the farm, including the
cow and her sweet calf! She was thankful that
Lydia didn't need her to return to the farm yet,
and pleased to think about how excited her
cousin would be when she learned about the
new quilt.

Caroline folded the letter. She started to
speak to the portly gentleman who was standing in front of her, eagerly reading his own
mail, when she spotted Mr. Osborne waiting in
line. He appeared to be fascinated by the floor-
boards, ignoring the commotion and avoiding
everyone's eye.

*It seems as if he doesn't **want** to be noticed,*
Caroline thought, although she couldn't imagine

why. She knew that none of the letters was addressed to him, and if he'd looked her way, she would have greeted him and explained that he didn't need to waste his time in line. But something about the almost stealthy way he approached the table made her pause.

When Mr. Osborne's turn came, he quickly looked over the letters spread on the table. He picked up one letter and slid it into an inside vest pocket. Then he turned and slipped away through the crowd.

Caroline stared after him, mouth open. Papa's friend had just stolen someone's mail! *I must tell Papa what I saw*, she thought reluctantly.

Back at the yard, she found Papa alone in the office, frowning over a sketch. "I have your letter..." she said, twisting her fingers together. "But, Papa? May I talk to you about something?"

Papa ran a hand through his hair, penciled a quick note, and turned around. "What is it?"

Caroline told him what she'd seen at the post office. "So when I saw Mr. Osborne steal—"

"'Steal' is a harsh word, Caroline." Papa's voice was stern.

Papa's displeasure made Caroline feel terrible—and confused. "But there were no letters addressed to him!"

"He might have been checking for someone else," Papa said. "One of the other workers here, perhaps."

"I know all of the men," Caroline protested, "and none of their names was written on—"

"That's *enough*." Papa frowned. "You could get Mr. Osborne into terrible trouble by making such accusations. What if someone started to suspect him of being a spy? Did you know that the punishment for spying can be prison, or even death?" He shook his head. "I'm disappointed in you, Caroline. Cyrus Osborne is my *friend*."

Caroline couldn't find anything to say.

"Now, if you please, I must get back to work." Papa turned away.

Blinking back tears, Caroline turned and left the office.

6
A Disturbing Message

After leaving Papa, Caroline headed for the dock. She sat down at the end with her back to the shipyard. Two workers were painting the trim on the gunboat anchored nearby. Beyond, navy men were at work on *General Pike*, and she spotted a navy patrol boat out on the lake. But was Sackets Harbor safe? Right this minute, a traitor might be giving the British information they needed to plan an attack on the village.

Worst of all, Papa's terrible words rang in her head. *The punishment for spying can be death . . . I'm disappointed in you . . . Cyrus Osborne is my friend.*

"But I'm your daughter," Caroline whispered. "And I was trying to tell you something important." She glanced at *Miss Caroline*, which was moored by the dock. *I wish I could just sail away in my skiff,* she thought.

Footsteps echoed on the dock behind her. "Caroline?" Rhonda called. A moment later, she sat down beside her friend. "I brought your sewing basket, since we need to leave soon for Miss Lucinda's house. But—is something wrong?"

Caroline told her what had happened at the post office and how Papa had reacted. "He got angry at *me!*"

"That must have hurt your feelings," Rhonda said, squeezing her hand. Two ducks paddled by, quacking as if they too thought Caroline had been treated unfairly. Finally Rhonda asked, "Why would Mr. Osborne steal someone's mail?"

"Several letters were addressed to navy officers," Caroline told her. "What if Mr. Osborne stole something important that was meant for one of them?"

"Mr. Osborne has been so friendly to all of

us," Rhonda mused. "It's still hard for me to believe he could be a—" She glanced over her shoulder. "A traitor."

"Our troubles started as soon as Mr. Osborne got a job at our shipyard," Caroline reminded her. "And he's always scribbling in his little journal. Maybe he's writing information about our gunboat and schooner. If the British learn how Papa designed the new boats, it might help the enemy attack them."

"I imagine the British also want to know when the new boats will be finished." Rhonda bit her lip. "We must be *very* careful, though. Before accusing Mr. Osborne of being a traitor, we must be *certain* of the facts."

Caroline's bones went cold as she imagined Mr. Osborne being arrested for spying. They froze altogether as she imagined Papa—and Miss Lucinda, too—hearing such dreadful news. "You're right."

Rhonda stood and shook wrinkles from her skirt. "It must be near time for our sewing lesson with Miss Lucinda."

As the girls started back along the dock, Rhonda pointed down at a rowboat moored beside Caroline's skiff. "What's that beneath the seat? It looks like a scrap of leather."

Caroline climbed down to the boat. "It's a sailmaker's palm." She turned the worn leather over and saw two tiny letters scratched into the back: *HB.*

"This belongs to Hosea," she added. "He must have dropped it while rowing out to stand guard on the gunboat last night. I'll return it and meet you in a few minutes."

Caroline joined Hosea and Paul in the sail loft. "I found something of yours," she told Hosea, holding out the palm.

"Why ... thank you, Miss Caroline," Hosea said. "I was wondering where that had gotten to." He pulled off the palm he'd been using and strapped his own in place. "Much better."

Caroline's mood improved a tiny bit as she ran back down the stairs. At least she'd done *something* good that day. "I'll go tell my parents that we're leaving," she told Rhonda. She hoped

A DISTURBING MESSAGE

Mama was in the office so she wouldn't have to interrupt Papa.

As Caroline approached the shipyard office, she heard a man's voice. "... soldiers searched him. They found a message written in cipher, hidden in the heel of one of his shoes. For God's sake, stay alert! These days are perhaps the most dangerous we've faced yet."

Caroline felt as if someone had poured a bucket of icy water over her head.

A tall man in a fancy navy uniform strode outside. She recognized Lieutenant Woolsey, the man who'd hired Abbott's to build gunboats when the war began. After he hurried away, Caroline stepped into the office. Mama was perched on a stool at the desk. Papa stood nearby, rubbing his jaw.

"Is there more bad news?" Caroline asked, too anxious to stay silent. "What's a cipher?"

"A cipher is a kind of secret code," Papa said. "Remember when Mr. Eckford told you about the spy caught in the navy shipyard? When soldiers searched his clothing, they found a note written in cipher hidden inside the heel of one shoe."

Caroline was relieved that Papa didn't seem angry at her anymore. "Can the navy men read the code?" she asked.

"Not yet, I'm afraid," Papa said.

Caroline felt a flicker of panic. "What if that note holds information about a British attack?"

Mama smoothed a stray curl from Caroline's face. "We're all worried about a British attack, but Lieutenant Woolsey is smart. He's putting out false stories about problems finishing *General Pike*, and he asked us to tell people that our schooner is behind schedule. He hopes the spies in town will hear that and tell the British."

Caroline thought about that. "So ... if the British believe the new ships won't be finished when expected, they may think they have plenty of time to plan an attack?"

"Exactly," Mama said. "We will hope and pray that the new ships—especially *General Pike*—will be completed while our enemies are still making preparations."

"You must not speak about shipyard business to anyone, Caroline," Papa added. "A spy might well try to get information from a child. Has anyone asked you questions about the yard lately?"

Caroline tried not to squirm. The only person who'd done that was Mr. Osborne! "I haven't talked about Abbott's to anyone who doesn't work here," she said finally.

"Good." Papa nodded.

Caroline sucked in her lower lip. She hated seeing her parents worried. She hated the anxious feeling churning in her stomach. She hated wondering if Papa's friend might be a traitor.

"Isn't it time for you to visit Miss Lucinda?" Mama asked. "Run along. A sewing lesson will take your mind off troubles."

But I don't want to take my mind off troubles, Caroline thought. She hoped that a quiet visit with Miss Lucinda would give her the chance to learn a little more about Mr. Cyrus Osborne.

When Caroline and Rhonda reached Miss Lucinda's boardinghouse, the landlady, a widow named Mrs. Simmons, pointed up a narrow flight of stairs. "Second door on the right," she said. "Not the first one! An officer's family has rented that one."

As the girls climbed the steps, an infant's wails came from behind the first closed door. "I don't think we'd have mistaken which door," Caroline murmured.

"Not likely," Rhonda agreed. She knocked on the second door.

Miss Lucinda opened it at once and beckoned the girls into her room. A bed took up most of the space. A stack of men's shirts, neatly pressed and folded, sat on top of a tall bureau.

"It's a bit cramped," Miss Lucinda said apologetically, "but I was lucky to find a room. Mrs. Simmons kindly provided a worktable too." Then she leaned closer and whispered, "Although I'd like thicker walls! I believe that poor baby next door is cutting teeth."

Caroline put her sewing basket down. "If the

noise becomes too trying, you could come sew at our house."

"That's a tempting offer," Miss Lucinda said. "I shall keep it in mind."

Rhonda pulled a drawing of a sloop from the basket. "Caroline traced this from one of her father's books," she said. "Will it suit for a quilt?"

"Perfectly," Miss Lucinda declared. "You can cut out the ship and sails from cloth, stitch them onto a background square of cotton, and then embroider the ropes and smaller details."

The worktable was soon covered with cloth. Rhonda cut out the paper ship, placed it on brown cotton, and traced around it with chalk.

As Caroline considered which piece of light-colored cotton to use for the sails, she was tempted to skip questioning Miss Lucinda about Mr. Osborne. *I wish we **could** simply sew this afternoon,* she thought wistfully. It would be so nice to forget about the war for a while! But every one of Miss Lucinda's sweet smiles was a reminder that Mr. Osborne—the man on whom she just might be pinning her hopes for a happy future—could be a traitor.

Caroline tried to think of a way to bring up Mr. Osborne. "Thank you for helping us. It's been hard to find time for fun."

"This war is a dreadful thing," Miss Lucinda agreed. She smiled sadly. "I'm glad my dear husband didn't live to see America and Britain at war again. He'd be deeply grieved." She paused, leaning over Rhonda's shoulder. "Be careful marking that point, dear. Make your lines sharp and crisp."

Although Caroline wanted to talk about Mr. Osborne, she couldn't help saying, "You must miss your husband very much, Miss Lucinda."

"I do," Miss Lucinda said simply.

"Well, perhaps you'll have another chance to marry," Caroline said. "Mr. Osborne seems quite taken with you."

Miss Lucinda's cheeks turned a pretty shade of pink. "Gracious, child. I—I have no idea what the future might hold."

A Disturbing Message

Rhonda shot Caroline a glance that said, *Don't embarrass the poor lady!*

"Does Mr. Osborne talk much about the war?" Caroline asked, still trying to shape the conversation. "Is he grieved, as your husband would have been?"

"Mr. Osborne and I," Miss Lucinda said, "try very hard *not* to talk about the war."

Caroline gave up the idea of fishing for information from Miss Lucinda. It was too hard! *I'll have to think of another way to learn more about Mr. Osborne,* she thought. At least now she could concentrate on the sewing project.

She was helping Rhonda pin the brown ship onto the background cloth when someone rapped on the door. "Lucinda?" the landlady called. "One of the navy men has come for the sewing."

"I'll be right down," Miss Lucinda replied. "Caroline, will you hand me those shirts?"

When Caroline picked up the shirts from the bureau, she noticed a necklace that had been resting behind them. The pendant featured a tiny deer carved from ivory. The cream-colored deer was mounted on a black stone, which was set into a gold frame.

"How pretty!" Caroline exclaimed. "Is it a family heirloom?"

Miss Lucinda's eyes grew merry. "Oh, no. Mr. Osborne gave the necklace to me yesterday. He said he found it at one of the market stalls."

Rhonda grinned. "That's very sweet."

"Indeed." Miss Lucinda accepted the shirts from Caroline. "I'll be back in a few minutes, girls."

When Miss Lucinda left, Caroline picked up the necklace. "I hope Mr. Osborne isn't—" She paused. She was standing beside the wall shared by the family next door, and she didn't want to be overheard. In a lower voice she continued, "It's hard to believe that someone bad could pick out such a lovely necklace." She looped the delicate gold chain through her fingers and let the pendant dangle so that her friend could get a good look.

"It's beautiful," Rhonda agreed. "Caroline, you simply must be mistaken about Mr.—about the gentleman. No one with a wicked heart could give a lady such a thoughtful gift."

Just then the baby let out a piercing shriek. Startled, Caroline jumped away from the wall. The necklace slipped from her fingers and fell to the floor.

"Oh *no*." She stared at the necklace in horror. The black stone was now sticking from the gold frame at an odd angle.

"Oh, Caroline, it's broken." Rhonda was staring too. "You should never have picked it up."

Caroline's vision blurred with hot tears. "It was an accident," she said miserably. She crouched and gently picked up the necklace.

When she inspected the damage, she felt a flash of hope. "I don't think it's truly broken," she said. "These tiny prongs hold the black stone to the gold frame, see? One prong must have gotten bent when it fell, and the corner of the stone popped loose."

"Can you fix it?" Rhonda asked.

"I think so." Caroline sat on the edge of the bed. "If I can just get the stone settled into the frame properly..." She pushed down on the black stone. It didn't budge. She pushed a little harder. The stone should simply slide back into the frame, but—it wouldn't.

Rhonda sank down beside her, twisting her fingers anxiously. "Don't do anything that might make it worse."

"I'm not." Caroline frowned, puzzled. "There seems to be a rough spot inside the frame, catching the stone when I try to push it back into place."

"Just let Miss Lucinda decide how to fix it," Rhonda urged.

Caroline tipped the pendant on edge and tried to peer beneath the stone. "Hand me a pin."

"A pin?" Rhonda looked confused.

"Please, just get it!" Caroline begged. Before Miss Lucinda came back, she wanted to see if something was blocking the stone.

Rhonda fetched a pin from the worktable. Caroline gently poked the pin between the gold frame and the back of the black stone. "Something is stuck in here," she whispered. She pinched the pin harder and wiggled it back and forth. When she felt the point catch on something, she used the pin to push it free.

"What is it?" Rhonda asked.

"Somehow a tiny scrap of paper got wedged in there." Caroline dropped the scrap into her lap and focused on the pendant. Now that the frame was clear, the stone settled neatly into place. She used one index finger to bend the loose prong back over the stone. "I fixed it!"

"And I'm putting it back where it belongs." Rhonda eased the necklace from Caroline's hand and gently replaced it on the bureau.

Caroline picked up the paper. The scrap had been creased. Once unfolded, it was no bigger than her thumbnail. But the paper wasn't blank. "Look at this!"

Rhonda squinted. "It's a string of tiny letters. But . . . they don't seem to spell anything."

"I think it's a cipher," Caroline whispered. Her mouth had gone dry.

Rhonda's eyes grew round. "A message written in code?"

"That's right," Caroline said. "Mr. Osborne must have hidden it there!"

"That doesn't make sense," Rhonda protested. "Why would he hide a message in the necklace? Why not just keep it in his pocket?"

"He's sleeping at the shipyard, so he doesn't have a speck of privacy," Caroline reminded her. "Maybe he's worried that the military men suspect him of spying for the British. If he gets arrested, all of his belongings will be searched. Hiding this in the gift for Miss Lucinda was *perfect*."

Rhonda's shoulders slumped. "This is just *horrible*. Should we tell Miss Lucinda that we think Mr. Osborne is a traitor?"

"Maybe I should show the note to my parents first," Caroline began. "But—no, wait." She remembered Papa's reaction when she had accused Mr. Osborne of stealing mail. She recalled what he'd said about spies facing harsh punishment. Finally she shook her head. "We haven't actually *proved* anything."

Rhonda thought that over. "I suppose that

Mr. Osborne could claim he had no idea there was a secret message hidden inside the necklace."

"We don't know who actually put it there," Caroline agreed. Suddenly she jerked upright. "I hear footsteps!"

By the time Miss Lucinda opened the door, the two girls were bent over their sewing. "Oh, this is going to be so pretty," Miss Lucinda said happily as she inspected their work.

"Thank you, Miss Lucinda," Caroline said. She tried to smile, but it was hard. That tiny bit of paper seemed to be burning a hole in her pocket.

7
Mysterious Sightings

"You girls are very quiet," Grandmother said that evening as the Abbotts and the Hathaways finished their supper.

Caroline exchanged a sideways glance with Rhonda. She'd had a terrible time pretending that nothing was wrong as they finished the sewing lesson with Miss Lucinda and as they helped Grandmother cook the meal. All this pretending was wearing Caroline out.

Papa said, "Caroline, did you notice the weather when you came in? It would be a fine evening for you and Rhonda to take the skiff out. There's a steady breeze blowing."

"There is?" Caroline glanced out the window. She'd forgotten about going sailing! From Rhonda's blank expression, she knew that her friend had as well.

Mrs. Hathaway looked uncertain. "So late in the day?" she asked.

"There are several hours of daylight left," Mama reminded her. "And the girls won't go too far. Isn't that right, Caroline?" she added meaningfully.

"Yes, Mama," Caroline promised. "We won't go too far."

After the meal, Papa walked Caroline and Rhonda to the shipyard. The skiff bobbed by the dock, and the girls were soon aboard. "Have fun," Papa called. He untied the mooring line.

"Will you help me row?" Caroline asked Rhonda. "We need to get away from the dock before I raise the sail."

Rhonda scooted to Caroline's seat and grasped one of the oars. "I'm glad to get away from everyone else," she said as the skiff wound past the larger boats anchored in the harbor. "Ever since you found that note written in cipher, my head has been jangling with all kinds of scary thoughts."

"Mine too," Caroline admitted.

"Where did you hide the note?" Rhonda asked.

"I sewed it into a handkerchief and buried it at the bottom of my worktable." Caroline made a long sweep with her oar. "I wish we knew what Mr. Osborne wrote in that note."

"We don't know for certain that Mr. Osborne is the traitor," Rhonda reminded her.

"I'm almost certain," Caroline muttered. "For all we know, he was even working for the British when he met Papa."

Rhonda thought that over. "Maybe Mr. Osborne just *pretended* to be a prisoner so that he could learn about American shipbuilding from your papa."

"Oh, Rhonda." Caroline stopped rowing. "What am I going to do? If we prove that Mr. Osborne is a spy, Papa will be miserable!"

Rhonda set her oar in its lock and rested, rubbing her hands. "I know," she said helplessly.

Caroline looked back toward Sackets Harbor.

She knew that since he'd escaped from the British, Papa treasured his family and friends more than ever. She often felt his gaze resting upon her, as if he was catching up on all the time they'd missed. She'd seen his fingers linger on Mama's after mealtime prayers. Sometimes, before giving instructions to his workers, he stood simply gazing over the shipyard with a look of pride and satisfaction.

And now, a friend he'd thought dead had reappeared. A dear friend ... who just might be a traitor.

"The work of one traitor might make the difference between winning and losing a battle—even the war," Rhonda reminded her. "We must try to discover the truth."

"I know." Caroline stiffened her resolve. "I can't accuse Mr. Osborne of being a traitor unless we find proof."

"I don't know how we're going to do that," Rhonda said glumly.

Caroline didn't know how they were going to do that either. She tipped her face to the sky and closed her eyes. She felt the cool breeze against her cheeks and heard the gentle slap of waves against the skiff's hull. Knowing that Papa had built the skiff, and that Hosea had stitched its sail, made her feel safe. Knowing that Papa believed she was steady enough to captain the skiff alone made her feel ready to face the troubles waiting back on land.

"We must keep a sharp eye on Mr. Cyrus Osborne," she told Rhonda. "We'll start when we get back to shore. Let's give ourselves a time limit for finding proof that he's doing something bad. Maybe . . . two days? If we haven't learned anything new in that time, I'll give Papa the note I found in the necklace."

Rhonda looked relieved. "That sounds like a good plan."

Their agreement made Caroline feel a bit better. "Right now," she said, "I think we should raise the sail and have some fun!"

Sailing *was* fun. It felt joyful to be away from the village, away from the work and worries, away from spies and ciphers and damaged supplies. Caroline waited as long as possible before turning around.

In fact, she waited a little *too* long. "Oh dear," she murmured when they'd gone about halfway back to Sackets Harbor.

Rhonda jerked up straight, looking alarmed. "What is it? Do you see a British ship?"

"No," Caroline assured her. "It's just that the wind is dying again."

She did everything she could to keep the skiff moving. Well before they reached Sackets Harbor, though, the wind died altogether.

Rhonda sighed. "Now we row?"

"Now we row." Caroline lowered the limp sail. Then she settled on the middle seat beside Rhonda, took a firm grip on one of the oars, and pointed the skiff for home.

It seemed to take a very long time to finish the trip. Purple twilight faded to full night. *Thank goodness the sky is clear,* Caroline thought.

The moon provided enough light for her to make out the trees and shoreline. She kept constant watch, searching for landmarks, making sure that they didn't mistakenly head for open water.

Finally the girls reached a marshy bay. "We're about a mile from Sackets Harbor," Caroline said. She paused to stretch. Her back and shoulders ached, and the palms of her hands felt raw.

"My mother will be worried," Rhonda fretted.

"Mama will know that the wind died," Caroline promised. "She'll explain that to your mother. Besides, we'll be home soon now." She scanned the shoreline once again and was surprised to see a flash of yellow. "Look—a light!"

Rhonda turned her head. "Where?"

"Right..." Caroline's voice faded away. "It's gone now. No, wait—there it is again!"

"Maybe someone is walking along the shore with a lantern," Rhonda said, "and we see the light blink as he passes behind trees."

"But the light isn't moving," Caroline pointed

out. "And the blinking is steady." On, off. On, off . . . as if someone were moving a shield of some sort back and forth in front of the lantern.

Rhonda leaned close. "Do you think it might be a signal?"

Caroline felt a squirmy feeling in her belly. "Maybe, but I don't want to row over there and find out." Not just the two of them, alone, in the dark.

"That light makes me nervous." Rhonda grabbed her oar. "Let's start rowing again."

"Yes, let's," Caroline agreed. "I'll tell Papa about the light when we get back."

The girls pulled the oars with renewed energy. Finally, *finally*, they approached the harbor. Caroline expected to see an American ship guarding the entrance, but no one challenged the girls. "The patrol ship must be down the coast a bit," she murmured to Rhonda.

In the harbor, a few pinpricks of light twinkled like tiny stars on the anchored navy ships. The masts of *General Pike* and several smaller boats were as dark as tar against the blue-black sky. "Almost home," Caroline added, still keeping her voice low. "Let me take both oars now."

"Gladly." Rhonda surrendered her oar. "My arms are all quivery."

Caroline rowed slowly into the harbor. They hadn't gone far when she heard a faint telltale splash in front of them . . . then another, closer yet. Caroline froze. Rhonda grabbed her arm.

Someone else was rowing on this windless night. *But that boat is heading **out** of the harbor,* Caroline thought. A shiver raced down her backbone. Why would someone leave shore at this hour, especially without a lantern?

Suddenly the village once again seemed far away. Caroline didn't know what to do. For several long moments nothing happened. The sounds had stopped, as if the person in the other boat didn't know what to do either. Peering around, Caroline made out a rowboat and the shadow of a single person. The rower sat hunched over, as if hoping to remain invisible.

Finally Caroline thought, *We can't sit here all night.* She scraped up her courage and called,

"Who's there?" Her voice stabbed the night like a blade. Rhonda flinched.

The other boatman didn't respond. Caroline sucked her lower lip between her teeth. If the rower was afraid to answer, he must be up to something bad! Was it Mr. Osborne? Had he found whatever information he'd been seeking? Was he trying to slip out of the harbor to pass that information to the British?

Then Caroline heard oars slice into the water again. The rowboat angled away from them. The splashes grew fainter, then disappeared.

Rhonda slumped with relief. "I think he—I think the boat's gone," she stammered hoarsely.

"Remember that blinking lantern we saw on the shore a little way back?" Caroline whispered. "Maybe somebody was waiting for a spy to deliver information."

"And when the man on shore heard us rowing past, he thought it *was* the spy, and that's why he signaled with the lantern," Rhonda finished. "Let's get moving, Caroline! I want to reach dry land."

"I wish we'd gotten a good look at the man in that rowboat," Caroline muttered. "But you're right. Let's go."

She threw another quick glance over her shoulder, wanting to be sure the skiff was still pointed toward Abbott's. Seeing a flicker of light in what seemed to be the right spot, she smiled. Was Papa waiting on the dock with a lamp to help guide the girls home?

But the flicker grew bigger, brighter, taller. Her heart leapt to her throat. "Rhonda, look!" she gasped. "Something at the shipyard is on fire!"

8
FRIENDS AND ENEMIES

By the time Caroline and Rhonda got the
skiff safely secured at Abbott's Shipyard, the
fire was out. The girls saw Papa, Mr. Tate, and
several workers near the dock, examining three
scorched barrels by lantern light. Caroline
quickly scanned the faces. The blacksmith was
there, and Paul, and Sam the rope maker as
well. Richard, the shipyard's caulker, was pacing
back and forth. Mr. Osborne was nowhere to
be seen.

Papa whirled when he heard their footsteps.
"Oh—it's you girls. I'm *very* glad you're home
safely."

"We are too," Caroline said. "We saw a
couple of strange things." She quickly described
the blinking light, and the rowboat she and

Rhonda had passed in the harbor.

"You girls did right to come straight home instead of trying to investigate on your own," Papa said. "Sam, run to the navy yard and report what the girls saw and heard. Then you can collect the girls and escort them home."

"Yes, sir," Sam said. He took off at a run.

Caroline gestured at the barrels. "What happened here?"

Richard hurled his hat to the ground. "My supplies were set ablaze, that's what happened!"

"The guards didn't see or hear anything?" she asked.

"*I* was on guard!" Richard exploded. "Paul and I. We walked a regular circuit. One of us passed this spot every five minutes." He muttered an oath. "All my oakum is ruined!"

Rhonda cupped her hands around Caroline's ear and whispered, "Please remind me what oakum is."

"Oakum is made from bits of old rope and the pitch from pine trees," Caroline whispered back. "When ships are built, Richard pounds oakum into every crack between boards so that water can't leak in."

"We can't afford another delay," Papa was saying. "Have we more rope ready to shred?"

"We do, sir," Mr. Tate said.

But it will take time to replace what was destroyed, Caroline thought.

Joseph, the blacksmith, spoke up. "I can shred rope tonight."

Caroline blinked in surprise. Tonight? But then... why not? "I will too," she said firmly.

"I can help as well," Rhonda added. Caroline squeezed her friend's hand.

Richard picked up his hat. "We'll get it done, sir." His voice was filled with resolve now.

Papa managed a small smile. "That's the spirit. Whoever is trying to slow down Abbott's crew doesn't know what he's up against!"

"We'll work here, back by the dock," Richard decided, "so we won't disturb anyone trying to sleep in the shop."

"I'm up next on guard duty," Mr. Tate said. "The damage has already been done, so I doubt we'll have any more trouble tonight, but I'll keep sharp watch. Since you lot will be back here, I'll patrol out front."

While the volunteer rope shredders were getting organized, Sam came back from the navy yard. "The officer I talked to sent soldiers to search the shore where the girls saw the blinking light," he reported.

Papa asked Sam to let Mrs. Hathaway and Mama know that the girls were back safely from their sail and that they planned to stay at the shipyard that evening.

"Please tell them we're *fine*," Rhonda added.

Caroline tugged her friend toward the carpentry shop. "Will you help me fetch some ... um ... supplies?"

Rhonda looked confused. "But Richard is—"

"Shh." Caroline put one finger to her lips. Then she grabbed a lantern and led the way.

The girls tiptoed into the dark shop. Caroline heard snores coming from a lean-to at the back. She crept around a workbench and lifted the lantern. The man sleeping had wrapped himself in a blanket, but a glimpse of carrot-red hair glinted in the lamplight. She cocked her head at Rhonda and led the way back outside.

"What was that about?" Rhonda hissed.

"I wanted to see if we could find Mr. Osborne," Caroline murmured. "But Mr. Osborne's hair is black."

"He may simply be visiting Miss Lucinda tonight," Rhonda said.

Caroline sighed. "You're right," she admitted. "Let's wait and see if Mr. Osborne comes to work in the morning."

"If he doesn't, we should talk to your papa," Rhonda said.

"And if he does show up," Caroline added, "we'll watch him every minute!"

Rhonda nodded. "We'll spy on the spy."

The blacksmith built a small bonfire. Richard dumped armloads of old bits of rope on the ground. Joseph and Paul sat on the ground and got to work. Papa sat down, too, and picked up a length of tattered rope.

Caroline and Rhonda settled on a log. Rhonda dug one finger into a thick piece of rope. "Like this?" she asked.

"Try to pull out just a few strands at a time," Caroline advised. "Otherwise your hands will wear out fast."

They worked in silence. The only sound was the crackling of burning logs. Then Caroline became aware of a sniffling sound coming from Paul's direction. The apprentice was bent over his work, but he paused to swipe at his eyes.

Caroline wished that Paul hadn't been on guard duty when the oakum burned. He already felt bad about being away from the yard when the sail had been slashed. Now he probably feared that he'd be blamed for this latest trouble.

Papa must have figured that out too. "How do you like sailmaking, Paul?" he asked. "Do you think you'd like to take charge of a sail loft one day?"

Paul hunched his shoulders in that shy way he had. "I do like the work, sir, very much. I—I think I could become a good sailmaker." He didn't look up, but Caroline was pleased. *Maybe in time Paul will forget to be so nervous,* she thought.

Papa began telling stories about his own boyhood adventures, and that made time pass quickly. After a while, Caroline leaned toward Rhonda and whispered, "I need to visit the privy."

She left the fire circle behind, rubbing fingers that felt prickly and tender from the scratchy rope. She didn't bother with a lantern because the privy wasn't far away. It sat in a back corner of the yard, near the woodlot where woodcutters dragged logs and sawyers left piles of planks, all waiting for the carpenters to put to use.

Several minutes later Caroline stepped from the privy, closing the door silently so that a sudden bang wouldn't alarm the men. She was just about to head back to the fire when a faint sound came from the woodlot to her left.

She froze. Had she imagined it?

Caroline peered into the shadows. The sound came again—soft as a sleeve brushing against planks, perhaps. A moonlit figure slipped between two of the stacks.

Goosebumps rose on her skin. Maybe Mr. Osborne was trying to sneak back into the yard! *This might be my best chance to catch him doing something suspicious*, she thought. Surely there was nothing to fear—not with Papa and the shipyard workers just a shout away.

Minutes ticked by. Then she heard a low murmur of men's voices. Mr. Osborne wasn't alone! Straining her ears, she was able to make out a few muttered words: "... too dangerous. I don't dare, not right now."

*Don't dare **what**?* Caroline demanded silently. Her heart skittered.

After a pause came the same forceful whisper, "*No*. There's a whole group working by the dock. Meet me here at four A.M. and we'll try again."

Caroline heard a faint rustle, as if one of the

men was slipping away. Or had both men left? She held her breath, silently begging Mr. Osborne to show himself. If she didn't get back to the fire soon, Rhonda or Papa would come looking for her.

Finally, her patience was rewarded. A man wearing a hat pulled low over his face leaned out into the open. He looked left and right, as if wanting to be sure that he and his friend hadn't been observed. Caroline pressed against the outhouse wall, trying to make herself invisible.

He seemed to conclude that all was well and removed his hat so that he could wipe sweat from his forehead. Before he disappeared back into the shadows, Caroline got what she wanted—a good look at his face.

She felt as if the blacksmith's hammer had just struck her chest. The man sneaking about the shipyard wasn't Cyrus Osborne. It was Hosea Barton.

Why would Hosea sneak about the shipyard? *Why?* Caroline might have stood by the privy for hours if a burst of laughter from the rope shredders hadn't startled her from her thoughts. She hurried back to the fire.

"I was starting to wonder," Rhonda said. "Is everything all right?"

"Fine," Caroline lied. "I just need to run over to the office for a moment." Ignoring her friend's puzzled look, she turned away.

This time she borrowed a lantern. Once in the office, she fetched the duty roster. Mr. Tate kept careful records showing each man's work assignments, including guard duty. Running her finger down the page, she found Hosea's name.

The day before, when she had visited the loft, Caroline had seen Hosea using his sailmaker's palm. Earlier today, she'd found Hosea's palm in the shipyard rowboat. She'd assumed that Hosea had lost it while rowing out to guard the gunboat in the harbor. But now, as she scanned the duty roster, her faith in Hosea turned to something hard as stone beneath her ribs. Hosea had not been assigned to the gunboat at all. He'd had no reason to be in the shipyard's rowboat.

Had Hosea been the man she'd heard rowing from the harbor earlier that evening? She remembered Hosea telling her that he'd asked for an apprentice. Having a helper would free up a little of Hosea's time and make it easier for him to leave the shipyard.

Maybe, Caroline thought, *Hosea is working for Mr. Osborne.* Hosea knew a great deal about the shipyard. And the two men had been on guard when the sails were slashed. Was it possible that Hosea had damaged his own work? Was he a traitor?

Hosea is my friend, Caroline thought. *I trust him.* But … hadn't Papa said the same thing about Mr. Osborne?

One thing was certain. Caroline needed to find proof. Before accusing Hosea of being a traitor, and if she could summon the courage, she had one good chance to do just that.

9
A Mighty Secret

At three o'clock the next morning, Caroline tiptoed out of her house and hurried toward the shipyard in the dark. She wanted to find a hiding place long before Hosea and his friend returned.

It was spooky to be on the streets at this hour. Once, she had to dart away from two sailors stumbling down the road, singing in off-key voices. *Maybe I should have asked Rhonda to come with me,* she thought nervously. But—no. Before telling anyone that she'd seen Hosea skulking through the shadows, she wanted to see what he was up to.

When she reached Abbott's, she didn't enter the yard through the main entrance. She was pretty sure that when the guards kept watch at night, they kept to the *inside* edge of the woodlot, where they had a better view of the shipyard.

Caroline tiptoed to the outside of the woodlot. Stacks of planks and logs created a maze of narrow corridors and shadowed spaces. In the starlight, she spotted a huge Y-shaped tree trunk lying near the edge of the lot. It might one day support both sides of a ship's hull, but now it created a perfect hiding spot. She slipped into the open space between the two arms of the trunk and crouched down. A few smaller branches remained on the trunk, with some dead leaves clinging to them. It didn't seem likely that Hosea would notice her there.

Time seemed to crawl. Caroline heard footsteps approach and fade away as the guards circled the yard. She heard the tiny rustlings of scurrying mice, and distant shouts as drunken men staggered from the taverns. Sweat trickled down her neck, and a mosquito bit her ear. Her legs tingled uncomfortably, then went numb.

Finally she heard a bell clang four times.

It's time, Caroline thought, peering cautiously over the log. She imagined Hosea creeping across the yard at just the right moment to avoid being spotted by the guards, and sliding silently between piles of planking to meet his friend.

Right on time, Hosea appeared not three feet from her hiding place. Caroline saw another shadowed figure approach from the other direction. His terrible limp identified him as the short sailor she'd seen laughing with Hosea in the marketplace three days ago. *A navy man*, she thought miserably. Was the sailor passing secret information to Hosea, so that Hosea could pass it to Mr. Osborne?

Despite the limp, the sailor joined Hosea soundlessly. "Now?" he whispered.

Hosea nodded. "We cut through here"— he pointed at one of the paths between stacked planks—"and slip to the dock. We'll have only moments to pass between the guards on their rounds. Be quick and be silent."

The men turned to go. Just then, a muscle twitched in one of Caroline's numb legs, jerking her off balance. Her hand hit one of the brittle leaves. The tiny crackle sounded like thunder.

Hosea whirled and pulled a knife that glinted in the moonlight. "Come—*out*," he commanded in a terrible whisper.

Caroline's heart thudded against her ribs. She couldn't move.

Hosea peered into her hiding place. His face was so fierce that she barely recognized this man she'd known all her life.

When he saw her, Hosea's expression changed—but just a little. He put one finger to his lips: *Stay silent.*

Caroline managed a jerky nod. Then Hosea and his friend were gone.

Caroline crept home again, feeling so hurt and bewildered that she scarcely noticed the shadows. *I must wake Papa and tell him what I saw,* she thought. But would Papa accuse her of carrying tales? And if he did believe her and take action, what would happen to Hosea?

One part of her mind argued that it didn't matter what happened to Hosea. There was simply no good reason to be sneaking through the shipyard at night, dodging the guards.

Another part argued that Hosea was a life-long friend. Despite the evidence, he might have some honest explanation for his actions.

By the time she reached her house, the only thing Caroline knew was that she wasn't ready to tell anyone about Hosea—*yet*. She'd known Hosea for too long to turn him in as a spy without giving him a chance to explain.

Heaven help me if I'm wrong to wait, she thought miserably as she tiptoed inside. The fate of the war might depend on her decision.

"Are you sure you want to go back to the shipyard this morning?" Mama asked Caroline over breakfast the next morning. "You girls have chores to do at home. Besides, you look tired."

Caroline poked at her oatmeal with a spoon. She *was* tired. She was also confused and frightened and heartsick.

After draining the last of his coffee, Papa wiped his mouth with a napkin. "If the girls want to help at the yard, we should let them. Goodness knows, we need every spare pair of hands."

"We'll catch up on chores, I promise," Rhonda added. "I was proud to help the men last night."

Beneath the table, Caroline pressed her knee against Rhonda's to say, *Thank you*.

Papa walked the girls to the shipyard. "I see that Richard left another mound of rope over by the barrels," he said.

"Caroline and I will get to work," Rhonda said. After Papa left to find Mr. Tate, Rhonda lowered her voice. "Look—Mr. Osborne is over there. He's working with two of the carpenters."

Caroline rubbed her sandy eyes. She'd almost forgotten about the plan to spy on Mr. Osborne.

Before she could answer, she saw Hosea approach. *He must have been watching for me*, she thought.

"It's good of you girls to help," Hosea said, sweet as cherry pie. Then he murmured, "Miss Caroline, will you please meet me by the fish sellers in the market at noon?" He walked away, whistling as if he hadn't a care, without waiting for a response.

As Caroline walked to the market at noon, her stomach felt twisted as tightly as the rope she'd left Rhonda trying to unravel. She spotted Hosea standing at a merchant's tent near the fish sellers, pretending to admire a pocket watch. "Thank you for coming," he said when she joined him. "Let's walk, shall we?"

Hosea ambled away from the tent, and she fell into step beside him. She was glad they'd met in such a crowded place.

"Have you told anyone about seeing me last

night?" Hosea asked under his breath. "Miss Rhonda, maybe?"

"No," Caroline replied. "But I will tell Papa if—"

Hosea interrupted her. "Miss Caroline, do you trust me?"

"I *used* to!" she hissed.

"Well, I trust you," he told her. "That's why I'm going to tell you a mighty secret, even though lives are at stake."

"*British* lives?" Caroline demanded, her tone hushed. "Is that why you've been sneaking about the shipyard at night? Have you been getting information from your navy friends and passing it to the British? Is that why I found your sail-maker's palm in the rowboat, even though you had no business being *in* the rowboat?"

"Please, Miss Caroline, try not to look so angry," Hosea begged. He tipped his hat at a woman selling flowers. "Let me explain. Then you can decide how you feel."

I already know how I feel, Caroline thought.

They'd reached the edge of the marketplace.

There were still plenty of people about, but Hosea steered them to a quiet spot against a warehouse wall where they could talk without being overheard. He took a deep breath before saying, "It's true that I've sometimes taken the rowboat out at night. I meet a British sailor on an island a few miles from here."

Caroline's heart fell like a stone tossed into the lake. She realized just how badly she'd wanted Hosea to deny everything.

"But I'm not borrowing the rowboat to carry information," Hosea continued. "I've carried several friends who have decided to join the British navy. George, the man you saw last night, was the latest."

"How could you *do* such a thing?" Caroline's voice quivered with fury. "You're helping our enemy! You've betrayed Papa, and—and *me*, and our country, and—"

"Hear me out." There was a hint of last night's iron in Hosea's tone. "George didn't *want* to go. He'd been in the American navy for over a year. He loved his job. He was proud to defend the United States, and he was willing to die doing so."

Caroline crossed her arms suspiciously. "So . . . why did he become a traitor?"

"Because the United States Navy was about to give him to a slave owner."

"What?" Caroline burst out. That made no sense. "But—but there are lots of black sailors in the navy!"

"The American navy welcomes the service of *free* black men." Hosea's face was calm, but a quivering muscle in his jaw betrayed deep emotions. "George is a runaway slave. He'd traveled so far that he didn't think he'd be discovered, but yesterday he spotted his master at the shipyard. George hid until dark, and then he came to me for help."

Caroline realized that she was wringing the fabric of her skirt in her hands and forced herself to stop. "No man should be held as a slave," she said slowly, "but still, to fight for our enemy . . ."

"George isn't fighting for our enemy," Hosea

told her. "George is fighting to defend *his* freedom. Just as America is doing." He glanced about, making sure no one had wandered close enough to eavesdrop. "You saw how badly George limps? Well, the injury that caused him to limp wasn't an accident. He ran away once before, and his owner punished him hard for it."

Caroline felt sick. *I didn't know,* she thought. *I didn't even imagine.* Part of her wished Hosea had never told her about George. But another part, the steady part, knew that she couldn't turn away from the truth.

"The British offer runaway slaves freedom, and a chance to live and work and die with dignity," Hosea told her. "United States law requires naval officers to return runaway slaves to their owners."

Caroline swiped at a tear. How could America's laws call for such a thing? Especially when the British offered freedom to runaways? "Well," she said angrily, "that law is stupid and horrid and just plain wrong."

"Yes ma'am." Hosea's voice was softer now.

"Oh, Hosea." Caroline looked up at him. "I'm sorry I suspected you of taking information about our shipyard to the British. It's just that everyone has been so worried about traitors, and I think that Mr. Osborne is keeping secrets, and—"

"Mr. Osborne?" Hosea rubbed the knuckles of one hand. "I've been wondering about your papa's friend myself."

Caroline blinked. "You have? Why?"

"Well, our troubles started right about the time he showed up," Hosea said. "And when he and I were on guard duty the other night, he disappeared for a while. I asked him about it, and he said that something he'd eaten had made him unwell."

"Hmm," Caroline said doubtfully.

"And my friend George saw him talking in secret with a U.S. Navy paymaster," Hosea added. "There's a spot beneath the bluffs on the far side of the navy yard where some of the black sailors gather sometimes to relax by themselves. Mr. Osborne and this paymaster have met at the same time for the last six evenings, right at dusk."

"Six?" Caroline said. She quickly counted back. "I met Mr. Osborne four days ago, and he told us he'd just arrived." She remembered his seeming mistake the evening he'd brought Miss Lucinda to the house—he'd given himself two extra days in the village. "Perhaps the paymaster is passing navy secrets to Mr. Osborne. It might be easier for Mr. Osborne to carry information than for someone in uniform."

Hosea lifted a hand to greet a friend trundling past with a cart of vegetables. "Maybe Mr. Osborne has borrowed a rowboat too." He gave a tiny smile that held no laughter. "It is possible to slip through the harbor after dark. I should know."

"Last night Rhonda and I saw a blinking light on the shore," Caroline told him. "About a mile away from the harbor. Perhaps Mr. Osborne rowed out to meet somebody who sneaks over from Upper Canada to get his messages."

"Could be," Hosea allowed. "And don't forget

the damage at Abbott's. Seems to me that the troublemaker is familiar with the yard—and the guard schedule, too."

Caroline put a hand on Hosea's arm. "You must tell Papa about George seeing Mr. Osborne meeting with that paymaster!"

"I can't do that, Miss Caroline." Hosea shook his head. "And you know why."

Her shoulders slumped. *Of course.* Hosea couldn't report what he'd been told without explaining how he'd come by that information. And that could betray his secret.

"I need you to understand something." Hosea held her gaze. "If *anyone* finds out what I've been doing, I'll be in mighty big trouble. Even worse, I wouldn't be around the next time someone like George needs my help."

Caroline nodded slowly.

"A secret this powerful is a heavy burden, and I hate to put it on your shoulders." He sighed. "After I saw you last night, though, I couldn't see any way around it. In a war like this one, where right and wrong can get all tangled up, we each have to answer to our own conscience."

*This war **is** all tangled up*, Caroline thought. Living right along the border between the United States and Upper Canada made it easy for spies and traitors to do their horrid business.

And what she'd just learned from Hosea only snarled things further. She studied her shoes, trying to decide what to do. It was shocking to think that experienced American sailors were joining the British navy. But it was even worse to imagine an American sailor like George being forced back into a brutal life of slavery.

Caroline looked Hosea in the eye. "Your secret is safe with me," she promised. "I won't tell a soul."

10

A DANGEROUS DISCOVERY

Caroline and Hosea walked back to the yard in silence. Caroline stared at passersby with new eyes. There were quite a few black sailors in Sackets Harbor. She'd assumed they were all free, just like the black people who lived in the village. How many were actually runaways? Her heart ached to imagine the anchor of fear they must drag about, every minute. And thinking about the risk Hosea took each time he helped a man escape to Upper Canada made her shiver.

But there was good news in all this too. Hosea was *not* a spy.

Caroline sighed as she considered that fact. Once again, everything pointed at Mr. Osborne.

At the shipyard, Caroline found Rhonda eating bread and cheese that Grandmother had packed that morning. Caroline plunked down on the log beside her friend, so close that their shoulders touched.

"What did Hosea want?" Rhonda asked.

"He told me a secret." Caroline hesitated, trying to find the right words. "Rhonda, I'd trust you with anything. But it's not my secret to tell."

Rhonda looked confused and a little hurt. Caroline understood—nobody liked being left out of a confidence! But finally Rhonda nodded. "All right. I won't ask any questions."

Caroline felt a wave of relief. "Thank you, Rhonda. Here's the important part. I learned that a friend of Hosea's has seen Mr. Osborne talking with a navy paymaster. They've met each of the past *six* evenings beneath the bluffs, where they're not likely to be seen. I suspect that the paymaster is passing secret information to Mr. Osborne, who passes it along to someone from Upper Canada."

"Can't Hosea's friend report what he saw?" Rhonda asked.

"No, I'm afraid not," Caroline said firmly. "So

it's up to us to find evidence that Mr. Osborne is a traitor. Did he leave the yard while I was gone?"

Rhonda shook her head. "He ate his noon meal alone, sitting down on the dock."

"Probably writing down information in that blasted notebook of his." Caroline reached for a sandwich. "We will keep watching Mr. Osborne."

The girls got back to work on the rope pile. As the afternoon wore on, if Mr. Osborne so much as walked into the carpentry shop to fetch a tool, Caroline shifted her seat so that she could keep an eye on him. He didn't do anything suspicious, though. By late afternoon, she was trying not to feel discouraged. *We'll have to follow him this evening*, she thought.

Suddenly a clanging bell startled her from gloomy thoughts. "Gather 'round," Mr. Tate shouted. "Mr. Abbott has something to tell you."

"Oh no," Caroline moaned. "I hope it's not more bad news."

She and Rhonda joined the workers as they assembled in the middle of the yard. The men looked uneasy.

"We've had some setbacks lately," Papa began. "So I'm especially proud to announce that the gunboat is ready for its trial voyage."

The workers grinned and whooped. Caroline clapped her hands. It felt good to have something to cheer about for a change.

"As you know, the new hull design was intended to permit the gunboat to travel very close to shore," Papa continued. "It's time to find out if we were successful. We'll head along the shallow marshlands east of here."

"Who gets to go?" one of the men called.

Mr. Tate started calling names. "Sam! Jed! Cyrus!"

When Mr. Osborne's name was called, Caroline gave Rhonda a worried look.

"I don't see what harm he could do on the boat," Rhonda murmured. "Not with all the other men along."

Caroline nodded. Surely even a black-hearted traitor wouldn't dare try anything evil while he was surrounded by loyal Americans.

The chosen men were already running to

the dock, jostling each other like boys let out of school. Papa paused by Caroline and Rhonda. "Why don't you girls accompany us in the skiff?"

"Oh!" Caroline bounced on her toes. "That would be fun!"

"Then you'd better get moving," Papa joked, "or our gunboat will be miles away before you get the skiff out of the harbor!"

✦

As it turned out, the girls didn't have to worry about being left behind. The men chosen to help test the new boat had to be rowed out from the dock. The gunboat was much heavier and slower than the skiff, too. Once Caroline reached the open lake, a brisk breeze filled the skiff's sail, and they quickly left the Abbott's crew far behind.

"This won't do," Caroline fretted.

Rhonda looked back toward Sackets Harbor. "We should wait for them to catch up."

Caroline lowered the sail again. For a few

minutes she tried to hold the skiff steady with the oars. Her hands were sore from rowing and rope picking, though, and the sun beat down without mercy. She soon felt restless.

"We're close to where we spotted that blinking light," she told Rhonda. "If the navy men who searched the shore last night had found anyone, I think we would have heard about it. Why don't we go explore while we wait for the gunboat to catch up? Papa said they'd be hugging the shoreline, so the gunboat will pass right by."

"That's a fine idea," Rhonda said. "We can cheer them along."

Soon Caroline was rowing through clumps of cattails with the skiff pointed toward a good landing spot. As they drew close, trees along the bank provided welcome shade.

Then the skiff struck something with a thud. "Oh!" Rhonda cried, clutching the seat.

"What did we hit?" Caroline demanded. "I didn't see a thing in the water!" She backed the skiff away. Once clear, she leaned over the side and frowned at something dark that rose just above the surface of the water, barely visible in the shadows cast by the trees. "It looks like a barrel."

"There's another one over there." Rhonda pointed. "No—two."

How strange, Caroline thought. "Maybe a supply boat got chased by a British ship, and the Americans threw some goods overboard to lighten their load and get away faster. Let's take a closer look."

She carefully eased the skiff back toward the closest barrel. It had come to rest upright on the sandy bottom near the bank. The barrel appeared to be tightly sealed, but there was a small hole in the top. A soot-smeared string rose from the hole, difficult to see in the shade. Keeping her gaze on the string, Caroline traced its path from the barrel to a shrubby thicket on shore.

"What are the strings for?" Rhonda asked. "All the barrels have them."

Caroline was baffled. "I can't imagine. These barrels weren't dumped overboard. Somebody placed them here very carefully."

She leaned toward the closest barrel and studied the hole. It looked just big enough for her little finger. She dipped her pinkie in the lake before sliding it into the hole beside the string. She felt something gritty, like sand. When she pulled her finger free, though, the coarse grains that clung to her skin were black.

"Oh *no*," Caroline whispered. The tiny hairs on her arms began to prickle. She suddenly had a strong sense that someone was hidden in the underbrush on shore, watching them.

She grabbed the oars, slapped them into the water, and heaved with all her might. "We have to get out of here!"

The sharp crack of a musket exploded the stillness.

"Someone's shooting at us!" Rhonda shrieked. A second shot was fired as they pulled away.

Caroline hauled on the oars. "I think someone is—just trying—to scare us away," she said between strokes. She hoped so, anyway. No musket balls had hit the skiff, and she hadn't heard any telltale splashes from near misses.

A Dangerous Discovery

As she angled the skiff back toward Sackets Harbor, a third shot cracked behind them. Her breathing came harsh and ragged as she strained on the oars. *Row. Row. Row.*

"Shall I help?" Rhonda asked.

Caroline gave one sharp head shake. Her arm muscles burned and sweat soaked her dress, but she didn't want to waste the seconds it would take to get Rhonda settled. *Don't—stop,* she chanted silently with every desperate pull on the oars.

And she didn't stop—not until she'd gotten *Miss Caroline* around a bend in the shoreline and out of sight from the marsh where they'd discovered the barrels. She dropped the oars, trembling. She didn't think she had enough strength left to lift a pencil.

"Raise—the sail," she gasped.

Rhonda's face was white, but she got to work. "Was that gunpowder in the barrels?"

"Yes." Caroline wiped her face with her sleeve. "And those strings were fuses. I think the person who placed those barrels was waiting for just the right moment to light the fuses. When we came along and took a look, he started shooting."

"Maybe he's following us on shore now." Rhonda threw a frightened look over her shoulder. She'd gotten the sail up, and the breeze caught the cloth with a satisfying snap.

Caroline straightened. Her heart was still racing, but there was no time to rest. "I don't think he's following us," she told Rhonda. "We aren't the target."

"What *is* the target?" Rhonda's voice trembled.

Caroline heard a shout up ahead. Abbott's fine new gunboat appeared in the distance, coming around a bend in the shoreline. Its sails were full, and the boat was traveling at a good clip, with Papa standing tall in the bow. Caroline had never been so glad to see her father— and so terrified.

"The *gunboat* is the target," she said grimly. "It was designed to travel close to shore, remember? Someone hidden in the woods back there is waiting to explode those barrels of gunpowder—and the gunboat with them."

11

A DESPERATE RACE

Caroline took stock of the wind and decided to take the skiff farther out from land to catch the full breeze. It was not the shortest route to the gunboat, but an extra gust or two would send the skiff speeding over the water.

Zigzagging back and forth to catch the wind, she used every speck of sailing lore she knew to reach Papa and his crew as fast as possible. *I must stop the gunboat,* she thought over and over. If she didn't, the gunboat—and every man on it—could get blown to bits.

While Caroline concentrated on sailing, Rhonda tried to get the men's attention by waving her arms wildly. When they drew nearer, she started yelling at the crew. "Stop! *Stop!*"

Several of the men waved back at the girls.

Mr. Tate, at the tiller, showed no sign of altering course. The gunboat raced along, close to the shore.

"They think we're cheering them on," Rhonda moaned. "You have to get closer!"

It's not that easy, Caroline thought. It was difficult to send the skiff *exactly* where she wanted it to go. She glanced frantically across the water, eyeing the distance between the skiff and the gunboat, considering the wind. She could drop sail and steer a straight course by rowing, but the gunboat would be long gone before she could catch up with it.

Caroline knew she had to make a decision, fast. "Slide over here by me," she commanded. "Watch out for the sail—I'm going to come about." Using their weight and the wind in the sail, she aimed the skiff on a course that would take it in front of the gunboat.

"What are you doing?" Rhonda cried. "We're going to collide!"

Caroline did not change her course. "Better a collision than an explosion."

A Desperate Race

As the skiff drew close to the gunboat, the men stopped cheering. Caroline glimpsed Papa trying to wave her off.

"Drop your sails!" Rhonda screamed to the crew.

Men leapt to do just that, but the gunboat had too much momentum to stop quickly. Workers yelled "Watch out!" and "Turn! Turn!"

Thank the heavens, Caroline thought. *We got their attention.* She kept her eyes on the gunboat bearing down on her little skiff. With a bit of luck, she and Rhonda might, just *might*, scoot clear. She leaned over one side of the skiff, trying to swing the smaller boat a few precious inches farther away and avoid calamity.

She *almost* succeeded. The gunboat grazed the skiff, which lurched sharply. Already off-balance, Caroline flew through the air and plunged into Lake Ontario. She felt the shock of cold water, heard oddly muffled thumps and yells and splashes, saw cloudy green blurs of movement. Within moments, her lungs felt ready to burst. Her skirt wrapped itself around her legs.

For an instant she panicked. Then a lifetime of her parents' warnings rang in her mind. She stopped thrashing long enough to look for the sky. Once she'd found it, she kicked her feet as hard as she could.

Someone appeared in the murky water beside her—Papa, his hair floating like lake weeds. He grabbed her arm in an oaken grip and dragged her up.

Caroline gasped when they surfaced, sucking air into her lungs, coughing. She pushed streaming hair from her face with one shaking hand. "Where's Rhonda?" she croaked frantically.

"I'm here," Rhonda called. She was kneeling in the skiff.

"Miss Caroline!" Mr. Tate leaned over from the gunboat, extending an oar. Papa shoved Caroline toward it. When she wrapped her hands around the oar, Mr. Tate hauled her aboard.

Several other men had jumped into the lake, too, but soon everyone was in the gunboat, and the skiff was tied alongside. Rhonda threw her arms around Caroline. "I thought you might drown!"

Papa's voice cracked like thunder. *"Caroline!"* He stood with feet braced, fists on hips, dripping and scowling. "What did you think you—"

"Please listen!" Caroline cried. Through chattering teeth, she quickly described the barrels of gunpowder that she and Rhonda had discovered. She saw Papa's eyes grow round with horror. "So I'm sorry," she finished, "but I had to—"

Papa crushed her against his chest in a hug. "Thank God you're all right," he whispered. "You saved us."

Then he looked at his workers. "Someone was expecting us. And no one knew that the gunboat was nearing completion and ready for trial except—" Instead of finishing, Papa turned his back on them all. He put both hands on the edge of the boat and hung his head.

Caroline's heart ached. She understood that Papa had been about to say, "No one knew that the gunboat was nearing completion and ready for trial except *Abbott's men*." A terrible silence fell over the boat.

"All right," Mr. Tate said at last to the crew. "Look sharp. We've got to get back to the harbor and alert the navy. They'll send men after whoever left that gunpowder and shot at the girls."

The workers jumped to obey. They looked shaken.

At least they're safe, Caroline thought, looking at the familiar faces—Richard, Sam, Jed... Suddenly she jerked upright. "Papa, where is Mr. Osborne?"

"What?" Papa raised his head. "Cyrus? He decided not to come along. He had an errand to run."

Caroline and Rhonda shared a glance. Had Mr. Osborne chosen not to participate in the gunboat's trial sail because he knew that something terrible was going to happen? The very idea took Caroline's breath away. What kind of person could pretend to be friends with these men and then send them to their death?

A traitor, she thought furiously. *That's who.*

She took a deep breath. "Papa? I must tell you some things about Mr. Osborne."

"Caroline," Papa began in a tight voice. Then he paused. "Very well. You've been smart and courageous today. What do you have to say?"

Talking very fast, Caroline told him about Mr. Osborne's little journal, the note in code hidden in the necklace Mr. Osborne had given Miss Lucinda, and a friend who'd heard that Mr. Osborne met with a navy paymaster every evening.

"Who is this friend?" Papa asked.

"A person who has worked at Abbott's for a long time," Caroline told him. "A person I trust. He's trying to help someone, and that's how he came to know about Mr. Osborne meeting the navy man. It's all a secret, and I *promised* that I wouldn't tell—but, Papa? I believe my friend is telling the truth."

Mr. Tate started shouting commands as the gunboat entered the harbor. Papa looked over the water. Caroline held her breath.

Finally Papa wiped a hand over his face.

"I have faith in my friend Cyrus," he told her. "But an hour ago I would have sworn that *none* of the men I employ could be a traitor." He drummed his fingers against his leg. "If time allows, you and I can go for a stroll beneath the bluffs this evening. We'll look for Cy and this paymaster fellow."

Caroline desperately hoped that they could catch Mr. Osborne in the act of passing or receiving information. The traitor had to be caught ... before he tried something even worse.

12

BETRAYED BY A FRIEND

As the sun sank in the western sky, Caroline and Papa began picking their way along the narrow, rocky lakeshore just northwest of Sackets Harbor. *This **would** be a good place for spies to meet,* Caroline thought. Tall limestone bluffs supported thick green shrubs that draped their branches toward the ground. Those rock walls formed sharp angles that kept anyone walking the beach from seeing very far ahead.

Papa walked in unhappy silence. As soon as the gunboat had returned to the shipyard that afternoon, he'd told navy men about the barrels of gunpowder. Officers had sent men to search the shoreline and collect the barrels. They had also questioned all the workers available. Mr. Osborne, however, had never returned to the yard from his "errand."

Rhonda had fetched dry clothes for Caroline and Papa. "Tell Mrs. Abbott that we had an unexpected dip in the lake and that we're fine," he'd instructed Rhonda. "I'll explain everything when I get home." Now, though, Caroline felt chilled despite her dry clothes.

"Take my hand," Papa said. They'd reached a spot where they had to squeeze between a jutting point of limestone on one side and lapping waves on the other. The stones between were slippery with moss, and Caroline was grateful for her father's firm grasp.

When she heard a low murmur of men's voices ahead, she tightened her grip. But instead of Mr. Osborne, Caroline and Papa came upon several black sailors playing cards in a sheltered corner. At the sight of Papa and Caroline, the men scrambled to their feet, their expressions suddenly guarded.

"Evenin', sir, young miss," one said. The other two touched the brims of their battered hats politely.

"Fine evening for a game," Papa told them. "My daughter and I are just out for a stroll."

The sailors stayed on their feet until Caroline and Papa had passed. *I hope that all of you are free men*, she told them silently. *And if not, I hope that the slave catchers never find you.*

She and Papa continued along the shore. Daylight was fading. A gull called overhead, and waves patted the rocks. Caroline bit her lower lip, worried that at any moment Papa would declare this trip a fool's errand and turn around.

Then they rounded another bend and saw two men huddled against the bluff. One wore an American navy uniform. The other was Cyrus Osborne.

Mr. Osborne looked up sharply, clearly alarmed. Then his face closed, just as the sailors' had moments earlier. "Why—I'm surprised—that is, I didn't expect to see you!" he stammered as Papa and Caroline approached.

"Clearly not," Papa said crisply. He turned to the navy man. "I'm John Abbott, and this is my daughter, Caroline."

"Paymaster Drake," the navy man said. Drake was a wiry man. He'd tied his gray hair with a ribbon at his neck. The look in his eyes reminded Caroline of Inkpot stalking a mouse.

"Caroline has something on her mind," Papa began, "and I thought it best we get everything out in the open. Daughter?"

Caroline took a little sidestep so that her shoulder rested against her father. Then she again described everything she'd discovered. When she mentioned that Mr. Osborne and Paymaster Drake had been observed meeting at the same time every evening for six days, they exchanged an unhappy glance.

"I'll pick up the tale from there," Papa said. As he described the barrels of gunpowder that Caroline and Rhonda had found, his voice quivered with rage. "And as the girls tried to leave, someone hidden onshore fired some shots."

Mr. Osborne gasped. "Good God, Caroline, are you all right?"

"I am," she said quietly. "But all of our troubles started when *you* came to work at the shipyard. Nobody except our workers knew that our gunboat was about ready for its first sail. And those barrels of gunpowder could have blown up the new gunboat—and every man on board."

"And you think *I'm* responsible?" Looking horrified, Mr. Osborne turned to his companion. "Say something!"

The paymaster held up his hands as if trying to calm Mr. Osborne. "Cyrus, I had no reason to think that something like this was being planned—"

"I want an explanation," Papa snapped. "*Now.*"

"I'll tell you what I can," Drake said, "but you must agree to hold what you hear in *strict* confidence."

Caroline nodded. "I agree," Papa said.

"Mr. Osborne and I are not traitors," Paymaster Drake said. "But we are spies."

Caroline narrowed her eyes. She didn't know what to make of that statement.

"My role of paymaster is largely a cover for my *real* work," Drake continued. "I came to

141

Sackets Harbor to identify and arrest British spies and American traitors."

Papa looked unconvinced. "And you, Cyrus?"

Paymaster Drake answered instead. "I approached Mr. Osborne a few weeks ago, after identifying a citizen I suspected of secretly working for our enemy. I asked Cyrus if he would come to Sackets Harbor and help me find proof."

"Why Mr. Osborne?" Caroline asked.

Mr. Osborne looked out over the lake. "Because I once knew the suspected British spy well."

"But who . . ." Caroline's mind raced. Unless Mr. Osborne was about to accuse Papa of being a traitor, she could think of only one other person who could be a suspect. *No,* she thought flatly. *It can't be.*

Mr. Osborne seemed to understand her confusion. "I'm afraid it's true," he said sadly. "Paymaster Drake and I were just discussing whether we have enough evidence to arrest Mrs. Lucinda Hodges."

Shadows were lengthening, but it was still

light enough for Caroline to see the pure misery
in Mr. Osborne's eyes. Papa put one hand on his
friend's shoulder. "Oh, *Cyrus*."

"The letter Cyrus took from the post office
was intended for Mrs. Hodges," Paymaster
Drake said. "I had learned the false name she
used for secret communications. A navy man
picking up a civilian's letter might attract
attention, so when the mail arrived, I sent
Mr. Osborne to look."

"And I did give that necklace to Miss
Lucinda," Mr. Osborne added, "but *she* must
have hidden the note inside."

Mr. Drake looked at Caroline. "I need the
note you found in the necklace, Miss Abbott."

"It's hidden at home," Caroline told him.

"Good." He nodded. "Two weeks ago I saw
Mrs. Hodges tuck something beneath a loose
brick behind one of the storehouses. It was a note
written in cipher, and I'll wager that the writing
and code match the note you found."

"Have you broken the code, sir?" Caroline
asked.

"We have, at last," Paymaster Drake said. "The note was clearly intended for a British agent. It provided information about the navy shipyard's progress with *General Pike*."

"But who has been making trouble at my shipyard?" Papa demanded. "Whoever was responsible knew where supplies were kept and how the guard system worked. I can't imagine Miss Lucinda creeping about unnoticed, or scurrying up to the loft to slash a sail."

"And who told the British about the gunboat being ready?" Caroline asked.

"We don't have all the answers yet," Drake told them. "But I am ready to arrest Mrs. Hodges. Let's hope she'll tell us what we need to know."

Caroline watched a blackbird walking along the shore. "It's so hard to believe," she whispered. Miss Lucinda was pretty and cheerful and—and nice! How could she have lied to them all? How could she betray her country? How could she help plan to blow up Abbott's gunboat?

"I know how you feel, child," Mr. Osborne said. "I came to Sackets Harbor intending to clear Miss Lucinda's name, but I've been forced to change my opinion."

"We must leave at once," Paymaster Drake said impatiently. "Mrs. Hodges might have discovered that the note she hid in her necklace is gone. If she fears that her true loyalties have been discovered, she may try to slip out of the village."

"I would like to be there when you arrest Mrs. Hodges," Papa said. His voice was hard. "I want everyone involved with those barrels of gunpowder to look me in the eye and face the truth about what they were doing. I imagine it's much easier to plot something like that when you don't have to see the intended victims of your treachery."

"You're welcome to come along," Drake said. "We'll take a couple of guards as well."

"May I come too?" Caroline asked. She understood how Papa felt. *Miss Lucinda didn't just betray our country*, she thought. *Miss Lucinda betrayed **me**.*

"I don't think a child—" Drake began.

Papa interrupted him. "Caroline might be

a child, sir, but she has acted with adult responsibility and steadiness. If it weren't for her—"
He cleared his throat. "She deserves to come."

Darkness had fallen over Sackets Harbor by
the time the little group reached Miss Lucinda's
boardinghouse. Paymaster Drake walked up the
steps with two armed guards. Papa, Caroline,
and Mr. Osborne waited by the street. Papa put
his hand on Caroline's shoulder, and she was
grateful. She felt quivery inside.

The landlady, lamp in hand, answered Paymaster Drake's knock. "Mrs. Hodges isn't here,"
Mrs. Simmons told him. "She went out about
an hour ago."

Oh no, Caroline thought. Had Miss Lucinda
managed to escape arrest?

Paymaster Drake walked back down the
steps. "I fear we've lost her," he muttered.
"She could be anywhere."

A baby's wail drifted from an open window

in the boardinghouse. Caroline suddenly remembered the offer she'd made to Miss Lucinda about a quiet place to sew.

"Papa!" Caroline grabbed her father's arm. "I know where Miss Lucinda might be!"

Caroline led the way through the busy village streets to the Abbott house. "One of you watch the back door," Paymaster Drake told the guards.

Caroline yanked open the front door and ran into the parlor. She found a peaceful sewing circle under way: Mama, Grandmother, Mrs. Hathaway, Rhonda . . . and Miss Lucinda.

They all jumped to their feet when the men clattered into the room after Caroline. "What on earth is wrong?" Mama asked, staring at Paymaster Drake and the armed guard.

"Perhaps Mrs. Hodges would like to explain," Mr. Osborne said.

Miss Lucinda smoothed her hair. "Why,

I don't know what you mean, Cyrus."

"I think you do." Mr. Osborne's voice trembled. Caroline wasn't sure if he was angry or sad. *Probably both*, she decided.

"Mrs. Lucinda Hodges," Paymaster Drake said, "you are under arrest for providing information and assistance to our enemy."

"What?" Rhonda said. Mrs. Hathaway and Mama looked shocked. Grandmother turned an icy gaze on Miss Lucinda.

The color faded from Miss Lucinda's face. "There must be some mistake."

Paymaster Drake looked at Caroline. "Fetch the note you found in the necklace, please."

Caroline carried a lamp up to her bedroom. Opening her worktable, she snatched out fabric and dumped it on the bed. She'd hidden the note, stitched into a handkerchief, at the very bottom.

The last bits of cloth went flying. Caroline gasped with disbelief. The handkerchief was gone.

13

CONFRONTING A SPY

Panicked, Caroline pawed through all of the fabric scraps again. No luck. How could the handkerchief have disappeared from her worktable?

I should have given that note to Papa as soon as I found it, she thought. The note was important evidence—and now it was gone.

There was nothing to do but go back to the parlor. Caroline forced herself to look Paymaster Drake in the eyes as she reported the theft. "I'm sorry," she ended miserably.

"This is complete nonsense," Miss Lucinda huffed. "Obviously the child is making up tales."

"I did *not* make it up!" Caroline protested.

"I saw it too," Rhonda added.

"Oh, Lucinda." Mr. Osborne shook his head. "You would cast blame on Caroline rather than take responsibility for your own actions?" He sounded ready to cry.

Everyone looked at him with sympathy— everyone except Caroline. Still angry at being called a liar, she glared at the seamstress. Miss Lucinda avoided her gaze, but Caroline noticed a tiny movement near the floor. There it was again! Miss Lucinda was using the toe of one shoe to nudge her sewing basket behind her chair.

Caroline ran forward, snatched the basket, and dumped its contents on a nearby table. Her handkerchief, carefully stitched closed, ended up on top of the pile. She handed it to the paymaster.

Drake held it up. "Just as you described, Miss Caroline," he said. Then he looked at Mama. "Was Mrs. Hodges ever alone in the house this evening?"

Mama shook her head. "No. That is— well, she did excuse herself earlier so she could slip outside and visit the privy."

Caroline suspected that instead of visiting the privy, Miss Lucinda had crept upstairs to search for the secret message. "She must have discovered that the note was missing from her necklace and guessed that Rhonda and I had taken it," Caroline said. "Miss Lucinda may have said she wanted a quiet place to sew tonight"—she looked at Mama, who nodded— "but what she *really* wanted was a chance to look for the note."

"I know you're not alone in this," Paymaster Drake told Miss Lucinda. "Whom do you work for?"

"I thought it was Mr. Osborne," Caroline added. "I almost reported *him* as the traitor!"

Miss Lucinda's shoulders sagged. "Cyrus had nothing to do with this." She gave him a pleading look. "I never meant to hurt you, Cyrus. I treasure our friendship."

"And yet you chose to betray my trust," he said sadly. "Who else is working against the Americans here in Sackets Harbor?"

She shook her head. "I can't say."

Papa stepped close to Miss Lucinda. "I daresay you *will*," he said furiously. "Is one of my workers a traitor?"

"I don't know which of your men is involved," Miss Lucinda insisted.

Caroline stamped her foot. *Someone* was collecting information and giving orders. "Who left those barrels of gunpowder?" she demanded. "Everyone on our gunboat almost got killed! Papa, and Mr. Tate, and—"

"What?" Miss Lucinda gasped. She pressed one hand over her mouth.

Mr. Osborne shook his head. "You and whoever you're protecting almost murdered innocent men today."

"I didn't know about that!" Miss Lucinda cried. "There *is* a spymaster in Sackets Harbor, but I don't know his name." She began wringing her hands. "Soon after I moved here, I received an unsigned letter. It said that I was known to have British sympathies, and that if I wished to help the British cause, I should meet a gentleman for instructions."

Paymaster Drake folded his arms. "So you *have* met this spymaster."

"Yes, but just once." Miss Lucinda's words came in a rush. "The night was dark—no moon, and clouds hiding even the stars. The man wore a big hat and a cloak. He gave me a code so that I could write in cipher. He told me that whenever I had information, I should leave a note under a certain loose brick."

"How did you come by this information?" Papa demanded. Caroline was wondering the same thing.

Miss Lucinda spread her hands. "Sometimes when I delivered the shirts I sewed, I picked up some bit of news about the navy." Her voice began to rise. "But when all this got started, I told the spymaster that I wanted no part in hurting civilians. And he said, 'Our goal is to destroy ships at anchor. Thundering thieves, woman, we're not—'"

"*Thundering thieves*?" Caroline interrupted. She clutched Papa's sleeve. "Maybe the spymaster is Mr. Growly—I mean, Crowley. You know, Mr. Eckford's clerk at the navy shipyard. He always says funny things like that."

Papa rubbed his chin. "That's hardly proof."

"No," Paymaster Drake said, "but it's a clue. Since he's one of the few people who knows everything about the navy shipyard, I've had him on a short list of possible suspects. Let's go have a talk with Mr. Crowley."

As one of the guards took Miss Lucinda's arm, Caroline planted herself in their path. All of her hurt and anger came pouring out. "I thought you were my *friend*."

"I'm sorry I disappointed you, Caroline," Miss Lucinda said quietly. "I truly enjoyed helping you and Rhonda with your quilt. I didn't know that you or your family would be put in danger."

"But—but how could you betray your own country?" Caroline persisted.

Miss Lucinda looked sad, but she lifted her chin stubbornly. "This is wartime, child. I always believed that we'd be better off under

British rule and that the American Revolution was a terrible mistake. This war gave Loyalists a chance to make things right. I had to follow my conscience."

With that, the guards led Mrs. Lucinda Hodges away.

Paymaster Drake followed them to the front door. "Let's go find Crowley," he barked. "Are you coming, Mr. Abbott?"

Papa turned to Mama. "I want to be with Paymaster Drake when he confronts Crowley. And I've told Caroline that she may stay with me until we see this thing through."

❖

Caroline held Papa's hand as they followed the military men and Miss Lucinda toward the navy headquarters. Caroline's thoughts were racing. She *did* want to see things through with Papa and the paymaster, but something else nudged at the back of her mind. When they neared the harbor, she looked up at Papa. "May

I wait at the shipyard instead?"

"But I thought..." Papa hesitated, looking from Caroline to Paymaster Drake and the guards, who were disappearing into the darkness. "Very well. But don't leave Abbott's until I come back to get you, all right?" He handed his lantern to her.

Caroline nodded. "I promise."

After waving to the man on guard duty, Caroline hurried toward the main building. As she approached, she heard footsteps pounding down the steps from the sail loft. A shadowed figure, short and slight, burst into the yard.

"Hey!" Caroline hollered. "Wait!"

Paul took off as if chased by wolves.

Caroline set her lantern on the ground, grabbed her skirt in both hands, and raced after him. Once he left the shipyard, he could find a hundred dark corners to hide in. *I can't let that happen,* she thought.

With every step Paul took, a leather haversack slung over his shoulder bounced. Just as he was about to escape the yard, Caroline flung herself at him and managed to grab the sack's strap. The two of them crashed to the ground.

"Ow!" Caroline cried.

"What's all this?" Mr. Tate called. He hurried over with a lantern.

Caroline scrambled up, brushing off her skirt. "I think Paul is a traitor!" she panted.

Mr. Tate hauled Paul to his feet. "Is that true?"

Caroline thought Paul might lie. Instead, all of the fight seemed to go out of him. "How did you know it was me?" he mumbled.

"When the troubles began here at the ship-yard, we had only two new workers—you and Mr. Osborne." Caroline scowled at him. "I thought Mr. Osborne was the troublemaker. But he's not. That leaves you."

Paul hung his head. "I'm sorry—"

"You're *sorry*?" Caroline sputtered.

Mr. Tate angrily grabbed Paul's leather sack. "And are you stealing from us now?"

"No!" Paul protested. He looked at Caroline. "Besides my cup and spare shirt, I have just the jackstraws you gave me and the sailmaker's palm Hosea helped me make."

The mention of Hosea just made Caroline's temper flare. "After all the kindness Hosea has shown you, how could you have damaged that sail?" she demanded. "And—and how could you watch the gunboat leave this afternoon, knowing that every man on board would likely be killed?"

Paul's eyes flashed in the lamplight. "I didn't know about the gunpowder until you all got back this afternoon!" he cried. "And now I'm trying to help make things right. I can prove it."

Late that night, Caroline and Rhonda sat on the bed in their room. A single candle cast a faint flickering glow.

"So Paul *was* involved in the spying," Rhonda whispered.

"He was born in Upper Canada," Caroline told her. She was exhausted, and everything she'd learned that evening was tumbling about in her mind, but she tried hard to explain what had happened. "After Paul's parents died, British soldiers gave him a place to sleep and some food in exchange for hard work. He dug privy holes and hauled firewood and scrubbed floors—things like that."

Rhonda reached over to pet Inkpot, who was curled on Caroline's lap. "I see."

"Paul said he didn't care about the war one way or the other," Caroline added. That was hard for her to understand. She cared so *much*!

"I suppose he was just glad for food and a bed." Rhonda sighed. "And I suppose it's no wonder that when a British officer promised to pay him to make trouble in one of the American shipyards, he agreed."

Inkpot began to purr. The mild rumble helped Caroline feel calmer. "Paul pitched the planks into the lake, and he burned the oakum," she continued. "But by then, he was getting to know everyone at Abbott's and starting to feel bad about causing trouble. Being ordered to slash the sail was the worst. He felt so terrible afterward that he tried to stop working for the British. Then he got a note saying that he'd get hurt or turned in as a spy if he didn't keep following orders.

"After getting that threatening note, Paul figured he *had* to keep working for the British. But when he heard that the gunboat had almost gotten blown up, he panicked and ran away. He was afraid of getting blamed for that."

Rhonda leaned back on her hands. "If Paul ran away from Sackets Harbor this afternoon, why did he come back?"

"He said that the farther he got from the village, the worse he felt," Caroline said. "He came back partly to leave behind that threatening note he'd gotten from the spymaster."

Rhonda shuddered. "Did the note come from Mr. Crowley?"

"Growly is the spymaster." Caroline didn't even try to call the clerk by his proper name anymore. She felt hot inside when she thought of the man who'd turned Miss Lucinda into a spy, and who'd threatened Paul. Worst of all,

Growly had been behind the gunpowder plot.

"Thank goodness he got caught," said Rhonda.

Yes, Caroline reminded herself. *At least he got caught.* When Paymaster Drake, Papa, and the guards had gone to question the clerk that evening, they'd found his cipher code hidden in his desk. With such strong evidence against him, Mr. Crowley had finally admitted to being in charge of all secret British activities in Sackets Harbor. "He was the person we saw in that rowboat last night," Caroline told Rhonda. "He was sneaking out of the harbor to meet a British agent waiting up the coast."

"Growly's note proves that Paul was trying to break his connection to the British," Rhonda said.

"And Papa says it's one more piece of evidence against Growly," Caroline added. "Even though he didn't sign it, the handwriting is his."

Rhonda nodded. "That makes sense."

"Paul had another reason for coming back." Caroline scratched the top of Inkpot's head. "He wanted to fetch his sailmaker's palm and the jackstraws I gave him. He said he'd never owned anything so special."

Rhonda was silent. Caroline was too.

How Paul must have treasured those simple gifts! she thought. He'd taken a terrible risk by coming back to the shipyard at all, for if the Americans *hadn't* been able to find enough evidence against Growly, the clerk might have successfully accused Paul of helping with the gunpowder plot. Caroline was grateful that Paul had returned—but she couldn't help still feeling angry at him, too.

She rubbed her eyes. "Let's try to sleep now," she said. Maybe tomorrow she'd be able to sort out her tangled thoughts and feelings.

14

CAUSE FOR CELEBRATION

A week later, another sewing circle gathered in the Abbotts' parlor. Miss Lucinda did not attend, but many of Caroline's friends did. A message had arrived from Uncle Aaron and Lydia a few days earlier: *Mrs. Parkhurst has found a new job and soon will be leaving our farm. We hope Caroline can return and help us through this busy summer season.* Knowing that they didn't have time to finish the quilt top, Caroline and Rhonda had asked their mothers and Grandmother to help. Soon word of the quilt project had spread. Neighbors and acquaintances had volunteered their time and talents.

At the end of the afternoon, Mama called for attention. "The quilt top is finished!" she announced. She and Mrs. Hathaway held the patchwork high for everyone to admire.

Caroline caught her breath. "It's beautiful!"

"It certainly is," Rhonda said proudly. "And the eagle block in the center is perfect."

"I think so too," Caroline agreed. She and Rhonda had chosen to discard the patchwork ship block that Miss Lucinda had helped them create. Instead they'd stitched an eagle—proud symbol of the United States of America. *And*, Caroline thought, *a symbol of our patriotic spirit*.

"Rhonda!" Amelia called. "Come see my block!"

When Rhonda joined her sister, Caroline stepped away from the group. Pleased as she was with the quilt top, she'd been feeling overwhelmed and confused ever since learning that Miss Lucinda and Paul—people she knew and liked—were traitors.

After a moment, Grandmother approached. "Why are you standing by yourself?" she asked. "I hope you don't mind that you and Rhonda needed help to finish the quilt top."

"We *had* wanted to make the quilt ourselves,"

Caroline admitted. "But, honestly, this is even better. So many people wanted to help—including some I never would have expected."

The biggest surprise—a pretty block made of tan and blue squares—had come from Hosea. "I heard you're working hard to finish a quilt for Miss Lydia," he'd told her the day before at the shipyard, when he handed over the block. "And I *am* handy with a needle. I whipped this up last night, after my other work was done."

Caroline gestured toward the group admiring the quilt top. "I love having Hosea's work in the quilt. And I'm grateful to all these ladies who helped sew the blocks together today."

"Women have a habit of knowing when to pitch in," Grandmother said. Her tone was mild, but her eyes held an invitation: *Is something else on your mind?*

"Just as Miss Lucinda pitched in to help the British?" Caroline asked bitterly.

"Miss Lucinda is a brave woman," Grandmother said. "Don't look so surprised! I do *not* agree with her beliefs. But I must admire any woman who is willing to take risks for what she feels is right." She nodded. "Like you."

That praise made Caroline feel better. "Our country isn't perfect," she said, thinking about Hosea and George and the horrid law that had sent them on their dangerous nighttime journey. "But I still want to do whatever I can to protect our independence."

"Of course you do!" Grandmother said briskly. "Now, I need to get back to the kitchen."

Caroline decided to step outside for a few quiet moments before rejoining the ladies. She was standing at her favorite spot, looking over the busy harbor, when someone called her name. Turning, she saw Papa approaching—with Paul.

As they joined her, Caroline found that she didn't know what to say. The military men had been holding Paul ever since the night he admitted to damaging the planks, sailcloth, and oakum at Abbott's in an attempt to slow down progress.

Papa seemed to understand her confusion. "Paul was released today," he explained. "Since he's been so cooperative and had actually come back to pass along Crowley's threatening note, the officers decided that a week in jail was enough. And," he added, "I decided to give Paul a second chance at the shipyard."

"A second chance," Caroline said slowly. The idea of having him back at the shipyard made her uncomfortable.

"When the British told me to slow down work on the schooner and gunboat, it seemed easy enough," Paul said. "But everyone at Abbott's was nothing but kind to me. I'm ever so sorry for what I did, Miss Caroline." For once, he met her gaze.

Caroline remembered the tears running down Paul's cheeks as he silently helped mend the damaged sail. "I guess you were following orders," she said grudgingly.

He looked away. "It purely broke my heart to take my knife to that sail."

Caroline felt the last of her resentment fade away. "I'm glad I caught you that night, before you could disappear again," she told him. "Do you still have the jackstraws?"

"Oh, yes," he assured her. "I've been practicing all week."

"Good," Caroline said. "I want to challenge you to a game, first chance we get."

"Perhaps this evening," Papa said. Then he put a hand on Paul's shoulder. "You go on back to the shipyard now."

"Yes, sir," Paul said at once.

Papa and Caroline watched him run back down the lane. Papa said, "He wanted a chance to apologize to you."

"That was nice of him," Caroline said. Not long ago, she would have hated *anyone* who helped the British. Now, she understood that every once in a while, things weren't quite so simple. She remembered something Hosea had told her: *In a war like this one, where right and wrong can get all tangled up, we each have to answer to our own conscience.* Hosea had done that. In the end, Paul had done the best he could to follow his conscience, too.

As Miss Lucinda had. Caroline gathered her

courage to ask a hard question. "What will happen to Miss Lucinda?"

"I suspect that she will be in prison for a very long time," Papa said. "Although she likely won't be punished as harshly as Mr. Crowley, who was directly responsible for all the spies working in Sackets Harbor."

Despite everything, Caroline was relieved to hear that Miss Lucinda's punishment wouldn't be worse. But there was something else she needed to say. "I feel terrible about suspecting Mr. Osborne. You trusted your friend, and you were right."

"Mr. Osborne trusted Miss Lucinda, and he was wrong," Papa reminded her. "Caroline, I can't promise that you'll never be betrayed by someone you trust. All you can do is follow your heart."

I followed my heart when I trusted Hosea, Caroline thought. *At least I was right about that. Still . . .*

"What's troubling you, daughter?" Papa asked gently.

"I can't stop thinking about those barrels of gunpowder," Caroline said. "Growly almost got away with his terrible plot!"

"I shudder to imagine what might have happened if his plan had worked," Papa agreed. "Thanks to you, though, all turned out well."

Caroline looked down over the harbor. The scene she knew and loved didn't seem quite so familiar anymore. "I never imagined that people I knew could be working for our enemy. Growly was always mean, but Miss Lucinda..." Her voice trailed away.

"I've thought about that too," Papa admitted. "If Miss Lucinda hadn't been caught, perhaps one day she would have decided that it was simply too difficult to work secretly against friends, just as Paul did."

We'll never know, Caroline thought.

"And as for Crowley," Papa said, "I wonder if he acted gruff to *keep* people from becoming friends."

"Maybe so," Caroline said. After all, Growly—unlike Paul and Miss Lucinda—had expected his schemes to have direct and deadly results.

Papa put both hands on her shoulders. "I'm very proud of you, Caroline. By acting quickly when you discovered the barrels of gunpowder, you saved the gunboat and all of us aboard. By thinking clearly, you helped us find Mrs. Hodges and Mr. Crowley. If we hadn't found Crowley in time, he might have tried to blow up *General Pike.* And Caroline—losing *Pike* could mean losing the war."

Caroline looked at *General Pike.* The great warship towered over the harbor, whole and defiant of British schemes. *Papa is right,* she decided. The ship was almost ready to launch, and that mattered most of all.

Papa nodded, as if he understood what she was thinking and feeling. "I've decided we should have a bonfire and picnic on the lawn this evening," he said.

"Will Mr. Osborne come, do you think?" Caroline asked. She hated imagining his broken heart.

"I told Mr. Osborne that he *must* attend," Papa assured her. "Learning that the woman he cared for was a traitor has been difficult for him. We need to remind Cyrus that he still has good friends in Sackets Harbor."

"I thought I might take him sailing in my skiff," Caroline said. "Being out on Lake Ontario helps me when I feel sad."

Papa smiled. "That's a fine idea."

"There you are!" Mama called. She came down the walk to join them, still holding the quilt top. "John, I didn't expect you home so early."

"We're having a party tonight," he said grandly. "I knew you'd want to thank your friends for helping with the girls' quilt. And I want to thank Abbott's workers. Not only did they build a gunboat I was proud to deliver to the American navy, but they also protected the shipyard—and my family." He put an arm around Mama's shoulders. "Did I mention that when Caroline ended up in the lake that day, half of the gunboat crew jumped in after her?

If Mr. Tate hadn't bellowed at some to stay put, there'd have been no one left on board to haul the rest of us up."

"They are good men," Mama said gratefully. Then she draped the quilt top around Caroline's shoulders like a huge cape. "Here you are, daughter. Once you reach the farm, you and Lydia can hold a quilting bee to finish it."

Caroline looked down at the colorful quilt— many different fabrics, many different patchwork blocks. Many hands had stitched them all together, making something beautiful and whole.

And many people care about me, Caroline thought. *People who are willing to take risks to stand up and do their best to protect American independence.*

"I'll put this away upstairs," she told her parents. She smiled—a real, happy smile—for the first time all week. "Then I'll help get ready for the party. We have a *lot* to celebrate."

LOOKING BACK

A PEEK INTO THE PAST

Sackets Harbor during the War of 1812

By July 1813, when Caroline's mystery takes place, America and Britain had been at war for more than a year. Caroline's home of Sackets Harbor, New York, was no longer a quiet little village—it had become the headquarters for the entire U.S. Navy on the Great Lakes. The British navy's headquarters were only thirty miles away, just across Lake Ontario in the colony of Upper Canada. Lake Ontario itself had become a key battleground in the war.

Both the American navy in Sackets Harbor and the British navy in Kingston,

176

Upper Canada, were working feverishly to erect forts, bring in troops, and build warships. Both sides were also trying hard to find out what the other side was doing! Having accurate information about the enemy could help a military leader decide exactly when, where, and how to attack. It could make the difference between winning and losing a battle—or even the war.

That summer, British spies in Sackets Harbor were looking for a way to destroy the nearly completed U.S. warship *General Pike*, the largest ship that had ever been built on the Great Lakes. The British knew that *General Pike* would give the Americans a big advantage, and they were desperate to keep it from sailing. In fact, spies really did hatch a plot to blow it up by using floating barrels of gunpowder, much like the barrels that Caroline discovers.

The great warship General Pike

A British general wrote this secret message on a tiny strip of paper, rolled it tightly, and hid it in the hollow stem of a quill pen.

Spies operating in Sackets Harbor could easily have snatched mail from the post office, just as Caroline sees in the story. And they probably did pass information written in *cipher*, or secret code, so that even if a message was discovered, Americans wouldn't be able to find out what the spies had learned.

No one knows whether a female spy actually worked in Sackets Harbor, but women spies were not uncommon. On both sides, women gathered military information and carried secret messages. Often, the British actually preferred to use women spies because if captured, they weren't searched as thoroughly as men and usually received a lighter punishment.

Just as in Caroline's story, some spies worked against their own country. In both

A British spy made this map of the Sackets Harbor area.

the United States and Upper Canada, there were many people who felt more loyalty to the other side. This was especially true along the Great Lakes and the Saint Lawrence River, which form the boundary between the two countries. Before the war, Americans and Canadians had often traveled back and forth to visit or do business, and settlers bought farmland regardless of which side of the border it was on. When war broke out, many people had to decide for the first time whether they felt more loyal to the American government or the British king. *Treason,* or betraying one's country, was common.

Americans could see Upper Canada across the Saint Lawrence River.

Laura Secord warning the British that Americans would attack

For example, an American named Laura Secord had lived in Upper Canada for many years. During the war, she spied for the British. Discovering that Americans would soon attack, she walked twenty miles to alert British forces. The British won the battle. Americans would have regarded her as a traitor, but to Canadians, she was a hero.

In May 1813, an American named Samuel Stacy betrayed Sackets Harbor. He told British officers when the village would be most lightly defended—and the British attacked at exactly that time, nearly defeating the Americans. Stacy was arrested for treason when he returned to the village in July to spy on American shipbuilding.

Many African Americans who had escaped slavery also crossed to the British side—but not because they were loyal to the king. They simply wanted to live in freedom, without fear of being captured by a slave

An African American family seeking a new home in Canada

catcher and forced back into slavery. Britain had outlawed slavery, so escaped slaves became legally free as soon as they set foot on British territory or boarded a British ship. During the War of 1812, more than 4,000 escaped slaves moved to Britain's Canadian colonies or joined the British navy.

Yet thousands of African American men fought on the American side. Most were free blacks. Escaped slaves did serve in the U.S. Navy, but, like Hosea's friend George, they were in terrible danger of being sent back into slavery.

Caroline would have seen many black sailors right in Sackets Harbor—almost

A black sailor during the War of 1812

one-fourth of the sailors stationed there were African American. Commodore Isaac Chauncey, who commanded the warship *General Pike,* wrote, "I have nearly fifty blacks on this boat and many of them are among the best of my men."

Black Americans who served in the U.S. Navy during the War of 1812 helped their young country win respect on the seas and among the nations of the world. Their brave service is especially moving because African Americans, whether slave or free, were not yet given the full rights of American citizenship themselves.

This painting shows black sailors risking their lives alongside white sailors in one of the most important battles fought on the Great Lakes.

ABOUT THE AUTHOR

 Kathleen Ernst grew up in Maryland in a house full of books. She wrote her first historical novel when she was fifteen and has been hooked ever since!

Today she and her husband live in Wisconsin. Her books for children and teens include the six-book series about Caroline Abbott and many American Girl mysteries, including *Clues in the Shadows: A Molly Mystery; Secrets in the Hills: A Josefina Mystery;* and two Kit mysteries, *Midnight in Lonesome Hollow* and *Danger at the Zoo.*

Kathleen has been nominated for the Edgar Allan Poe Award and the Agatha Award, the nation's top awards for children's mysteries.